Painkiller Ghosts

Painkiller Ghosts

J. Marc Harding

Library of Congress Control Number:		2010901911
ISBN:	Hardcover	978-1-4500-4214-7
	Softcover	978-1-4500-4213-0
	Ebook	978-1-4500-4215-4

To order additional copies of this book, contact:
Xlibris Corporation
1-888-795-4274
www.Xlibris.com
Orders@Xlibris.com
75942

CONTENTS

PART ONE:
Amateur Photojournalism,
A Name, & Thyme's Other Bygones

PART TWO:
Shooting You Is the Closest
I'll Get to Sleeping With You, No Name,
& Other Feel Goods

PART THREE:
Photography, Unemployment, & Otherwise Popping Pain Pills

PART FOUR:
As Momma Lay Dying, Three Pennies, & Other Daydreams

PART FIVE:
Unemployment Pills, a Trespasser, & Other Daymares

Part One

Amateur Photojournalism, A Name, & Thyme's Other Bygones

Prologue: [Endings]

She Had Brown Eyes, But That Was Years Ago

There was a time, before he was shot (again), before Chastity was framed in his camera's lens, before that No Name body fell from the sky (seemingly), when he was Thymothy and he was in love, but in need (of help, of direction), but that was years ago.

They had a past; there was pillow talk about the future.

And they felt healthy.

He remembers that feeling.

Her name was Maria, and she had brown eyes, but that was years ago.

The first thing she told him about herself was: "I love water that tastes like purple French roses." But that was a long time ago, and now, looking back, he can't remember her ever drinking rose flavored water, but definitely purple French red wine. She had brown eyes, years ago.

This is five minutes ago, two years ago: she's dead.

This is ten minutes ago, two years ago: and she's dying, counting tiles on the floor, off by one. She's on the floor. She's sinking into the linoleum, barely feeling the echoes of her heartbeat. She's confused, but knows she's in her home. A new echo in her ears moans, confusing her more, and she's trying to count the floor tiles, and she's off by one, then two.

The floor feels warm and then doesn't feel at all. She's feeling good.

It was too much this time.

She's on the floor that used to be white, and then became tan over time, and now is stained brown with just a footprint next to the sink.

She's dropped a needle onto the floor.

She's looking at the dead bulbs and not seeing them.

She died counting the tiles on the brown floor, and was off by one, two.

She couldn't remember what color eyes he had; she couldn't remember their dog died months ago.

He is barefoot in the living room, stumbling. (Numb.)

He's stumbling, breaking an ashtray. He has burns on his fingers, sores, jagged toenails. He's got cobweb hair; he's a bearded skinny skeleton in a shirt, three pennies poor.

He's thinking a little about the dog, the one that's gone. He remembers what color eyes the dog had; he knows what color eyes Maria has. (Had.)

He goes to the front door, stumbles near it, closes his eyes for one second, two, and then makes sure the bolt is latched. Constantly, the bolt is latched: someone is in the hall, waiting for him, waiting to get in. (One hundred are waiting.) He hears breathing, footsteps. (One thousand are waiting.) He hears them. (Shadows hiss.)

He hasn't left in days. (Old calendars.)

He has blue eyes. (Red and blue.)

He's on the sofa again now. (Dust on the cushions.)

The television is on. (Dust on the screen.)

He does it and wants to do it again. (Sweet dizziness.)

When does the dog get fed? (Memories melt.)

He can still hear that jingle, the jingle of the tags on the collar. That dirty collar, the one that he buried with the dog months ago, months and months ago. (Death melts.)

He looks at his watch, although he doesn't care what time it is. It wouldn't matter anyway. He's wearing a dead watch; she gave it to him and the battery died when the dog died and he hasn't taken it off since. (Time melts.)

He finally goes into the bathroom in the morning. (Dust in the shower.) He's blinded briefly by the bulbs and then he sees her, on the floor. (His life.) He doesn't cry. (Dehydration.)

He turns the lights out. (Two bulbs.)

He goes to the phone. (His hands are shaking.) He calls the emergency number. (Ingrained since childhood.) He tries to talk, but coughs. (A little blood.)

"She had brown eyes, but that was years ago." (His, now red.)

Then he leaves their apartment, leaving the bolt unlocked for the first time.

He leaves and wanders around aimlessly and ends up at a friend's apartment. He sits down.

Hours pass by.

Days pass by.

Weeks pass, and he's weak. And sick.

Weeks pass by and he goes to his mother's house; he's a mess. He goes home to kick, to sweat in the bed he used to sleep in when his eyes were blue and clear, but now they're red and blue, with a little white; a tattered American flag.

That was two years ago, and now he can't remember if her breath used to smell like rose flavored water or not, but he likes to pretend that it did.

Chapter One

An Erratic History of Thyme, Part One

When he was born, he was six pounds, almost, and bald.

He was born a bald skinny skeleton, and he smiled until socks were put on his feet, then he screamed, and peed on his nurse. He opened his eyes wide, stretched his arms out as far as he could and grabbed at the socks, missed, tried again, missed again, and instead of a third try, he promptly fell asleep for two minutes before waking up screaming and grabbing at the socks again.

For her blue-eyed darling boy's birth certificate, Suzanne Exler did not provide a father's name; she named her son Thymothy Exler. He was born a couple weeks early and his mother hadn't decided on a middle name, so she put an X.

Thymothy X Exler.

None of Suzanne's children had blue eyes, and she can't remember sleeping with a man with blue eyes, recently. She didn't want her son to know who his father was, or probably is. She'll explain it all to him, one day, and he'll be glad he doesn't know.

He was a fourth child to his unmarried mother, by as many men, probably.

Suzanne Exler had her first child when she was eighteen. She named him Wylde. He lived to be eighteen before he died driving headfirst into a tree. (Oak.)

She had her second child at age twenty-two. It was a daughter named Mississippi, and everyone called her Missi. Missi drowned in the same river she was named after on her twenty-second birthday. (Vodka.)

She was twenty-five when the next child was born, a son named Gatyr. Gatyr put a bullet in his head (a .45) the same week that Thyme (then still Thymothy) was shot by Maria's father (a .38).

Her last child was Thymothy X Exler. He has lived the longest. (She was twenty-six when he was born.)

None of the children knew their fathers, but their mother knew who the fathers were, except for the father of Thyme. Father Thyme is unknown, and both Thyme and his mother could care less. The only thing that she ever wonders about is where Thyme got his blue eyes from.

By the time that her blue-eyed son moved back home at age early thirty-something, emaciated, dark hollows under his eyes and sorrow in his tone, he was her only child. By the time Thymothy came back home, to sleep in the days only to stare out the window in the middle of the night, she knew that she couldn't lose another child.

Suzanne has basil-green eyes; all of her children had brown eyes, save Thymothy. Now, under her roof, are her fifty-something eyes looking into her son's thirty-something eyes, red and blue. Almost like the flag. But they were beautiful; striking even. Years ago, that is. Her eyes were white clouds with fresh herbs; her smile is a celebration with charisma.

And now Thymothy's blue eyes had the blues, with a layer of white around them. Red, too. Red scratching through the white. He talks in his sleep. His frown is obvious through his beard.

Suzanne will go to work in the morning and come back during the six o'clock news. She lets him sleep all day. She makes sure she locks the doors and windows, his paranoia can be paralyzing. She would persuade him to shower, or she would just sit next to him as he stared at the television. She would read the news from her laptop screen aloud, trying to get a reaction out of him (a nod here and there); he'd go to bed and toss and turn for hours. (Swimming in sweat.)

When he did dream, he'd talk to himself and scream here and there and Suzanne always heard it but he was trapped in the past. (Entombed.)

Days went by. (Hours melt.) Days and days. (Weeks melt.)

He finally woke up one day without a headache, with less of a heartache, and looked out the window, wondered what day it was, what month it was, and then went down to the kitchen, where his mother was eating her breakfast, and he sat down next her.

And smiled.

Thymothy X Exler was called Thymothy for thirty-something years.

However, this morning, after coming down to breakfast, he looked Suzanne in the eyes and told her he wanted to be called Thyme from now on, not Thymothy: Thyme.

"Thyme," his mother repeated, "I like it, I do. But why the change?"

"Because that's all I got, Momma, time's all I got now."

He says to Suzanne, "You've lost another son, Momma. I'm sorry, but Thymothy is dead, he has to be. I'm only Thyme now."

"I understand, son."

"Completely dead, Momma. Disregard any mail for Thymothy, throw it out. Tell phones calls for Thymothy that he's dead; they're mostly creditors anyways."

"Thymothy's defunct."

This was the last time Suzanne ever said the name Thymothy aloud.

He began to get up earlier and after a few months he was able to sleep through the night; he went outside and walked around one day, and then the next.

He began to get up in the morning when his mother did and have breakfast with her: soy sausages and tea, headlines on the laptop, National Public Radio on the air. He'd talk to her until she left for work: she'd make a guess about gas prices, a smear against a politician, and then she'd be out the door, and so would he, with sunglasses on and a camera around his shoulder.

The air smells so good.

He's missed the sharp gravel feel under his bare feet. He's missed feeling the concrete's warmth. His camera becomes his constant companion.

Chapter Two

Snapshots of Suzanne

Thyme, at the breakfast table the next morning, says to Momma: "I think I'm going crazy."

"Why's that, Thyme?"

"I've been hearing things."

"Things?"

"Noises. Last night I got out of bed and walked downstairs to open the front door to let the dog out."

"What dog."

"That's right, that's what I'm saying. I got up and walked down to the door and I opened it and stood there for a minute, looking at the moon, and I even think I heard a collar. Then I closed the door and I felt happy. It was weird, it was a weird feeling. I felt better, but I also felt like I had seen a ghost, but I didn't see anything at all."

She blows on her tea, listens to the news on the radio until the next story starts, one she's uninterested in, and puts her hand on Thyme's hand, and says, "You're not crazy; there are things we don't comprehend, that we don't see. But it's okay; you just have to accept it."

"Accept what?"

"That you don't understand."

"Oh." He stares at her, blankly.

"Thyme, let me ask you this."

"Shoot."

"You said you felt better, after doing that, hearing it last night."

"Right."

"Do you know what I call things like that?"

"No; what?"

"Painkiller ghosts."

"Oh. Thanks, Momma."

"You're welcome. I need to go, to work; I'll be out late tonight, don't wait up."

And she walks out of the front door and he can hear her gun her engine and hears a horn honking and then he hears her horn and her tires squeal on the street and it is just another morning for Momma, and Thyme is still in the kitchen wondering if he's lost his mind, and thinking about painkiller ghosts.

Thyme's mother's eyes are the color of the newest ivy sprigs in April.

She's had rich lovers and starving artists. One father of her children was a businessmen; another was a sculptor saving every dollar for cigarettes or maybe the electric bill.

She drives fast and enjoys surviving car wrecks, not the cheapest of thrills she knows, but the cracking glass and the screaming, twisting metal makes her giddy. She wakes up early to drink yerba matte, she likes to smell it as the sun comes up; she likes to drink three cups before she leaves the house.

She reads mystery novels, and then throws them in the fireplace when she's done. In her spare time, Saturday mornings, Sunday evenings, she works on her own mystery novel, typing on her laptop, typing a mystery to become someone else's fireplace fodder.

She knows what it's like when a man falls in love with her. And that's the time when she knows she must get rid of him. Tell him not to come back, not to call her cell.

She was never disappointed by any of her children; they all at some time fell in love and assumed she would be disappointed; they'd known her to avoid it all their lives.

Thyme points out, one morning, that all of his siblings thought the same thing: "We just assumed that you thought we'd be weak, or were weak, since we were in love."

"Why would you think that, honey?"

"I don't know, Momma; it's just that none of us ever wanted to disappoint you."

"And none of you did. Ever."

She says, "I think that love would make me weak. It makes some people strong, but I just haven't found the love in me yet. Maybe one day I will. We can all be wrong, right? Maybe I'll change one day."

Thyme thinks, 'She had brown eyes; but that was years ago.'

Suzanne has her own ideas about pain, and regret, and remorse, and she believes in killing painful memories with smiles, she believes in painkiller ghosts. She misses a lot of people; she wishes she could hear some of those people again, their voices, their sneezes, just the sound of someone's keys being thrown onto the counter.

Momma hopes Thyme will be able to find his own path to painlessness.

It can be a long road.

Momma's mother had died thirty-some years ago; the cause was never clear. She and her father haven't spoken in more than half that time; she'd try to send him a Christmas card once in a while and it always came back 'return to sender', unopened. She thinks he's moved; maybe to a trailer in southern Alabama, but he hasn't been seen since Katrina. He's gone by now she feels; either by that storm or just age. He'd be over eighty by now, and never ate well and smoked and drank too much; over the years, she just assumed that he was gone and she thought that would be the best thing for her, and for her kids, to just act like he was dead, even if he wasn't.

In airports, especially when she used to travel a lot, she always scanned the local obituaries for his name.

But what if she'd found her father's funeral announcement, in an airport, on an April afternoon, awaiting a flight to Atlanta: would she exchange her tickets? No. No, she wouldn't. But she doesn't spend too much time thinking about that, about fathers, and definitely not too much energy.

She's forgotten what her own father looks like, looked like; she knows she should know, it's just that she doesn't want to remember. She just doesn't care. But sometimes she ponders if her father is dead; she wonders: does he wander? Does he wander around this area, where she was a little girl, and he would walk up and down this very sidewalk to work, change clinking together in his pocket (and she remembers when he would get home from work, walking home after dark, and she, Suzanne, would run to meet him, and she'd hug him, and then hold out her hands, and he'd empty out the pennies that were the change from the lunch he had bought somewhere, and she'd run off, counting her pennies, and show her dolls, and then she would hear her mother say Hello to her father, but that was back when her mother was alive, and her father was, too.)

Suzanne likes having a man touching her.

The men come over, they come, and they go. She locks the door when they leave, turns off the front light before their car starts.

She likes it like that; she likes her tea alone the next morning; she likes to have the whole bed to herself; she doesn't want a man to wake her in the morning looking to do it again. Not before her shower, not before her cable news.

The men will tell her that when she brushes against them, they feel like kings. One glance from those green eyes melts them. And she knows it.

She doesn't mind them falling for her, but she tells them she won't love them. It just doesn't happen.

She enjoys the company, for a while.

Often, one man is smitten in the foyer, undressing, another is texting her, telling her he's coming over.

She drives her car fast.

She drives Thyme around when she has the time. She says, "If time's all you have now, Thyme, I'm not going to let you waste it by driving slowly." Every few weeks she'll say this again like it's the first time she thought of it (and he'll feign like he's never heard it before): "Thyme, if there's one thing that I know, it's that you were conceived in one of my cars. It wasn't moving at the time, I doubt, though maybe, but you were made on a noon drive, it was a beautiful day, the sky was blue, we were taking the turns faster than ever.

"That might explain your blue eyes."

Besides time, blue eyes are all he's got now, and three pennies of course, three pennies poor.

Chapter Three

An Erratic History of Thyme, Part Two

The first time he got too close to a fire was the time that Maria's father shot him.

The first time that Thyme was shot he was still Thymothy and he was shot by Maria's father, with a .38 handgun, in the left shoulder.

Maria's father meant to shoot someone else. Thymothy was not the target; the target was someone who was wrestling with him, with a knife at his throat, near flames, hidden by thick smoke.

The entire night was a confusing one, especially for aiming a gun.

They were visiting her father at his house in Mobile, in early 2001, before those big hurricanes hit, and she had been looking forward to seeing him.

They had been there one night; one and a half days really. They were down for a week and had driven her car there. Maria's father still worked as a policeman in the city, and he figured he'd do it a few more years.

While her father was at work, Maria and Thymothy were at a park reading, kissing, and smoking a joint. Later, back at her father's house, Maria sat down on the couch to watch the news, Bush was in his first months in office, the world was calm, the weather was calm, the celebrity rehabs were full; he went outside to light the charcoal in the grill. He came in and took a shower while the grill warmed up; she fell asleep on the sofa. Her father came home and he quietly called his sister up in Oxford.

Thyme had finished his shower; Maria's father went up to shower. Thymothy opened a beer and went to the grill to prepare dinner. He had his beer, and a paperback book.

Through the open bathroom window he could hear her dad singing in the shower, the radio tuned to the oldies channel. He found himself laughing aloud while trying to read to the off key singing, and found himself repeating paragraphs. Thymothy grilled; Maria's father sang and showered.

Then there was a great crash, from inside, a shatter, collapsing glass, that cracking noise.

A scream.

He dropped his book, bounced towards the door and didn't realize he knocked over the grill, with his paperback lying under some red burning charcoal, the spilt plastic container with lighter fluid, leaking out onto the door jam.

He pounced through the door, ran in the living room where Maria was catnapping peacefully five minutes before. There was a man on top of her. They were wrestling, falling off the sofa, shattering a glass table. The man had a handful of Maria's hair, and a knife near her breasts, a little blood seeping through her shirt. He cut some of her hair with the knife and tried to stuff it into her mouth.

Thymothy ran over and kicked the man in the side of the ribs, then rammed his left knee into the nearest cheek; a tooth was spit out. Maria was coughing, bleeding, trying to crawl away, gagging. By the time Maria's father turned off the shower, the first thing he smelled was the smoke. Naked, he ran to grab a fire extinguisher and that's when he saw Maria crawling on her elbows away from a man who was fighting Thymothy.

He ran to the coat closet, for his gun.

By the time he reached the living room again, the carpet was on fire. A man had Thymothy on the ground, pinned in an awkward half-nelson with a knife to his neck.

Maria's father yelled for the man to back off, drop the damn knife.

He was coughing, the gun was not steady, and there was smoke in the air. Thymothy was on the ground, and the man began to cut him, the knife was slicing into his throat.

Maria's father aimed the gun to the stranger's head, which was the best shot he had.

Instead the bullet sank into Thymothy's shoulder, who yelled out in pain. The man dropped Thymothy, thrown off by the shot. The gun fired again. The knife was heading towards Maria, the man leaping for her.

The drapes on the window were on fire.

He fired a third shot, hitting the man in the lower part of the spine, who fell towards Maria, screaming profanities.

Thymothy was in shock, pain.

The man shoved Maria towards a burning window drape and ran with the knife towards her father's chest.

Next door, the neighbors called 911.

Her father fired again, twice in a row, putting a bullet into the Adam's apple, and then kneeing the man down onto the floor, but the man with a frantic burst put the knife into Maria's father's stomach.

The flames got larger.

Sirens were getting closer, a fire truck, two. Maria heard the sirens down the street, but she shut her eyes for a second.

Maria awoke in the hospital unharmed more or less save a few bruises, burns, and a stitch, or ten.

Her father's house had burnt down and her father had died from an infection from the stab wound and smoke inhalation.

The intruder had died right alongside her father, not ten feet from where her hair lay, on the carpet, burning.

Chapter Four

Why Her Brown Eyes Were Blue

Thymothy awoke in the hospital.

It was in Mobile, at the hospital, that Thymothy discovered morphine. He spent five days on it in the hospital.

At home, Maria went back to work. But Thymothy's arm was still healing and he couldn't go back to working as a carpenter. He tried two pain pills at first, then a little more than recommended, and he'd try to sleep through the day waiting for Maria to get home. She made him feel better. Only her, really. And pills.

He told himself that he wasn't using the drugs to get high; he had pain.

But they did get him high. Confused at first; mellow later. Starting in the stomach, a deep warm feeling. It starts there and spreads to his legs, which then start to itch. Especially the left one, the left one itches first.

Maria would take some of his pills; "I'm in pain, too" she'd counter.

She blamed herself for her father's death. He was trying to protect her, to save her and Thymothy. She had never asked him for anything; but then, never really had given him anything either.

She blamed herself for Thymothy getting hooked. She told herself that if he hadn't have gotten shot, he wouldn't have started on the morphine; if he hadn't had to take time off of work he wouldn't have been walking all over the city looking for hook-ups.

The wound never got back to how it should have been, and he never worked in carpentry again.

He had jobs sometimes after that, here and there, after he was shot, but a lot of times he didn't have one; sometimes he'd sell some weed here and there, paint a house here and there. Maria's father had tried to save his daughter's life, Thymothy's life, and he did, and never knew it.

The first time this bearded skinny skeleton was shot it was by Maria's father, and while the wound would heal eventually, the scar will always be there, that taste of pain pills never leaves the memory, the back of the tongue, where it's a tattooed taste.

Thyme can never change that.

But this is really why her brown eyes had the blues:

Sometimes in the night, with Thymothy asleep next to her, she'd wake up and get sick. He'd be resting, sweating, right next to her in boxers and a white t-shirt. She'd wake up, stroke his beard, snag a hair now and then in a nail and he'd stir his head but not wake up. High. Very high.

She was chewing codeine while having sex; shooting up when she should have been having breakfast.

She was pregnant, for a little while.

Then the dog died, too.

She never wanted to be pregnant. She lost her child before he ever knew of it. She thought it was a little girl. She could never stop thinking that it is a girl in there. Was.

She would wake in the night, see him sleeping there, stroke his beard, get up, and vomit in the toilet. The two bulbs burning were her only confidant. She'd get up, brush her teeth and then walk in sock feet down the hall back into the bedroom, open the drawer where they keep the stash, and go back into the bathroom.

And she, Maria, got depressed, felt like she had turned black on the inside and her brown eyes had the blues and her hands had the shakes and she was sick.

And when the dog died, she didn't know if Thymothy was going to be okay. She worried about him. The dog died and then all he did for days, a week, was stare at the wall, with glazed eyes, and he looked like he had suddenly gotten the flu. He knew he was stuck in some kind of sadness, but couldn't get himself out for a while; and the whole time Maria was dealing with her own inner death feeling, and he didn't even know anything about it, and wondered why she was acting so distant to him at a time where it was obvious that he needed her.

And now it's now, and this is how it is: Thyme is in bed. He fell asleep quickly, thanks to a longer than usual walk, and he quickly falls into dreams.

He dreamed he was awake in his back yard, or some back yard at least, and he was dreaming of a backyard that was near a lake (although he never lived in a yard near a lake) and he had some friends over (although he's never really had friends for years) and the sun was going down, and it was autumn, and the sky was orange, a bright, burning orange, and he's throwing a tennis ball to his dog, the one he misses so much but who is alive now, in this bright orange dream, and he's alive (the dog) and now he (Thyme) feels alive and he's throwing the ball for his dog, who's wagging his tail, and Thymothy (not yet Thyme) is laughing and throwing the ball and Thymothy's friends are there, singing, passing joints around, and there's Maria, with her beautiful eyes, and she's smiling at him, calling out to the dog, their dog, and laughing, smoke clouding her face. And then someone panics, a few people, and Maria too, because above them, in the orange and pink sky, a plane, on its way to the airport not too far away, has started to shake and slow down in the air and everyone at Thymothy's party started to look up into the sky, to point, to stop the laughing and the singing, and Thymothy heard someone say, 'Hey, that plane's gonna crash!' and it was silent and the engine sound in the sky died, and it was silent, so silent; the dog stopped chasing the ball, and sat on the ground, the cold hard ground, and then laid down and stared at the sky, at the plane falling. But then, then the most beautiful thing happened, they heard it, the crowd did, the party did, they heard that engine sound start up again, and they looked in the air, and the plane started to fly again, to gain altitude again and started to head back into the air, instead of plunging with a crash onto the ground; and everyone cheered; the dog smiled and started chasing its tennis ball again, and the plane flew out of sight, and there was silence.

And so the party started again.

And the joints were passed around again; and the dog was barking and playing again; and Maria was blowing into Thymothy's ear again, and then the sound of another plane came over the water, over the lake that was behind the dreamland house, and the crowd began to cheer, the party began to cheer, the dog dropped its ball and stood next to Thymothy and wagged its tail and barked while the people cheered and held their cups up into the air and Maria was blowing kisses at the plane and people were smiling and then all of a sudden this plane, this second plane burst into flames and then dropped down as a fire ball into the lake in front of the party, Thymothy's party, and flames fell from the sky, and then when the plane hit the lake, the ground shook, and kept on shaking, even long after the plane had fallen and floated as burning wreckage on the lake, the earth kept on shaking, and everyone in Thymothy's party was shouting, and burning, and that's when Thyme woke up.

And the next day, he watched the news all day long, just to see if he had dreamed the crash; and the next day, when he was out walking and heard a plane pass over in the sky, he felt ill at ease, and watched the plane until it was out of sight and not a burning wreck falling on him.

Chapter Five

Photography, Loneliness, and the Never Ending War

This is now, and this is what he thinks about: A couple of years ago he was without time and he was someone else, now time's all he's got. Thyme's time. He buried his girlfriend, but not really. He was in too much of a daze to go to her funeral. He has dreamed about it, the funeral. Her eyes, brown and beautiful, are gone now; six feet underground and seeing nothing, dreaming nothing. Sometimes in his dreams he sees her eyes, but most of the time he forgets what she smelled like, what she felt like, forgets if she actually drank rose flavored water. That was all years ago. She had brown eyes, but that was years ago.

He's put on a few pounds, no longer quite the skinny skeleton. He didn't have dreams for two years after he moved back into Suzanne's house. It was like sleeping in a car, that feeling he'd have the next morning; he sleeps in his bed for eight or nine hours straight, and wakes up feeling tired and confused, with a sore neck.

He can never remember his few dreams; the ones he does remember all bother him, so he prefers not to dream.

He never picks up the phone to call old friends from school; they all have families, or jobs, not even jobs, no: occupations, careers. Thyme has none of it. He has no money, no resume. He'd do small jobs here and there, but nothing too heavy, nothing that paid too heavily either.

Momma Exler is his social life for the most part.

Sometimes when he's outside, barefoot and drinking tea, he talks to the garbage men: a guy about Thyme's age and his father, Conroy & Son Refuse Service. He and the son get along; Father Conroy, on the other hand, always looks at Thyme, and sighs. Conroy, Jr., tells Thyme, "Don't mind him; he always looks at whites funny. You should see the way he looks at your mother."

"Momma?"

"Oh, hell, he don't mean a thing."

Thyme takes over the grocery shopping for Suzanne (she'll make the list and provide the debit card). At first, Thyme would go into the store shoeless, and every time he would be asked to leave. He'd walk the half mile back home, take about ten minutes finding a pair of shoes, and head out down the sidewalks again.

One manager is a woman a few years older than Thyme, named Erin.

He's met Erin before, twice briefly, back when he was Thymothy; it seems like such a long time ago.

Now, after seeing him in the store once or twice, Erin has tolerated him, even befriended him a little, and allowed him to shop barefoot, but swore that if he stepped on a broken bottle the store was not to blame. Thyme smiled. He picked up a scrap of paper, and wrote a sentence accepting responsibility, and signed and dated it, and handed it to her. She smiled back. He was only allowed to go barefoot in the store on the days when she was the manager. She'd give him her schedule; he'd tell Suzanne that they'd be out of eggs until the next day, no way did his feet want to put on shoes today. Then Thyme and Erin would talk while he was shopping (vinegar, sweet corn, baby spinach, veggie burgers), but they never really mention meeting each other, the first time, they both let the recognition go silently.

Thyme asks Erin for a job.

She doesn't answer for a minute.

"I don't know, Thyme."

"Please; I'm not the kid that I used to be. That was Thymothy, the one who was wild. I'm Thyme."

She closes her eyes, thinking, and finally says, "Okay, Thyme, you get night shift."

He smiles, "That's what I wanted."

He works at the store three nights a week, stocking shelves after the customers leave; he gets there at quarter til ten and leaves about half past two, give or take.

He only works at nights, so he can be barefoot ("If I can, I will.").

Even though his eyes are blue, dazzling, they still seem scattered, distant. He seems to be at odds with himself. Erin notices. Erin knows Thyme's mother by sight. She asks about Thyme when she sees Suzanne. Momma

Exler thanks her for giving Thyme a job, a reason to leave the house, she says, "Even if it is the graveyard shift."

Thyme watches television. A recession channel. A weather channel. A war channel. A war on drugs channel. He flips a channel: prisoner abuse; on another everyone seems to be in foreclosure; and what is a recession anyhow? There are seventy two channels, and he can never find a good show.

When he was high (on bitter white pills, on junk), he'd stare mindlessly at the screen and not really be watching it, not really be realizing what was going on. He remembers seeing the planes fly into the towers. Not real at all to him. The grey smoke floating up, seen miles away. The people on camera caught choosing between burning and jumping; often jumping. Nothing seemed real to him at the time. The dog died too, eventually. So did Maria. But now, now it's all seeming real to him.

He tried to lose himself in television; he didn't have enough concentration to watch a movie, but had enough to stare at the news hypnotized for hours. He never really thought much about the mountainous region between Pakistan and Afghanistan, but the photojournalists and their camera men tell and show Thyme the world. Photojournalists were getting kidnapped, beheaded. The world that had stopped being real to him at one time was right there.

He'll have to change the channel now.

He'll find himself staring at the reality shows. Renovation shows, selling houses shows. Shows about rocks stars, blind dates, people that can't clean out their own garages. Cooking shows; exercise shows; rehab shows; intervention shows.

Then he'll dream all night of the war, the wars, the bird flu, the swine flu, some new flu, or some good looking woman he saw at the store, and the pot plant he has growing, hidden in the backyard. He dream a lot about that plant, sticky sweet leaves, but he'll forget about his dreams, the bad and the naked, before he starts his first cup of tea the next morning.

Thyme has his mother and he has his beard; he has his night job at the store.

He has a credit card with a debt he won't be able to pay off for a long time, and a credit history he hopes someone would steal.

He has a bullet scar. He has a joint in one hand, nothing in the other.

He has time. And sometimes he's got hope.

Thyme visited Maria's grave once. Twice, actually. He went, decided he couldn't stand it, and left. He got less than a mile away, then turned and went back. His mother found him there in the morning.

He wouldn't speak for two days after that. He sat staring at the war channel on the dusty screen all day.

For a day or two, he remembered what she smelled like, laughed like, how she sneezed every time hot sauce was around, how she would cough on bong hits, smiling; he's trying to remember her drinking her rose flavored water, freezing rose petals into ice cubes to float around in the purple, rose flavored water.

Later, Thyme found his high school yearbooks, photo albums with pictures of him and his underage friends drinking cheap beer, girlfriends in jeans and bras. He threw them all out. He flipped through them all, smiled, and tossed them in the trash with the empty cartons of free-range chicken eggs. He threw out all of his old shirts. He threw out his old art, his old photography. He tossed out anything in his desk drawers that had been there for more than six months. He cut up his credit card, though he doubted it worked anyway. He quit smoking cigarettes on the front steps and while on breaks at work.

He walks daily. He never takes an iPod, never takes a cell phone; he likes to hear the sounds around him, natural and otherwise.

He walks in the early morning, and he walks in the late evening.

He looks forward to working in the store those three nights a week, sometimes covering for someone else and going there four nights. He laughs to Erin about how he used to hate to go to work at a grocery store when he was sixteen. He used to hate to be a bag boy, packing produce, taking them out to the cars of old people. He hated having to go from the chilly air conditioning to the blistering hot pavement; he hated the gas fumes. In the winter, it was the opposite, he'd be freezing outside and go in and sweat under his jacket, but couldn't take off the jacket because he had to turn around and walk into the cold breeze again with more bags of produce and canned goods.

But now, he tells Erin, he loves to be alone, stocking the shelves barefoot, listening to the metallic clinks of cans, the shifting sounds of the dry dog food, the hiss of the sprinklers on the produce coming on and off, on and off, ice machines booming in the seafood department every fifty-three minutes, and he's alone, stocking six different brands of canned kale, barefoot, and happy.

Happy.

Chapter Six

An Erratic History of Thyme, Part Three

The first time is the time that brings that rush to your head, which won't be there the next time. The first time, what you do is look both ways, grab it, and run, not making eye contact, trying to get lost in the alleys. The first time robbing someone that is.

But you have to run. Fast.

And that's what Thymothy did, he ran. Ran. Ran and smiled, laughing all the way through parked cars, overgrown city backyards, down an alleyway with abandoned Lazy Boy chairs, curious dogs barking and peeing.

He couldn't resist it; he couldn't stop himself. Afterwards, he felt good, real good. He felt high.

He was in high school. It was a Saturday evening in late March, when it seemed that winter was not too long gone, and spring not too far away.

The first time that Thymothy robbed somebody, the first time he pulled a gun on a couple walking home through an alley, he got what he wanted. He got enough to fill the tank with gas, find someone buy him a six-pack. The first time that Thymothy pulled that gun on the couple he knew it was a good idea.

He pulled the gun on a man and a woman, they were only about five years older than Thymothy was it looked like; the two were close, he had his arm around her shoulder and she was laughing and smiling and they saw Thymothy up a little ahead of them in the alley but they just thought he'd keep on going.

He pulled the gun out, and the man stopped talking, but the woman said, "Oh, what? Come on, don't."

But he did; he kept the gun there, pointed right at them, until they handed over the money that they had in their pockets and wallets.

He tried not to say much. (A statue.)

He tried not to be human. (A hyena.)

He tried not to have feelings. (A thorn.)

And he didn't think about them as people. (A virus.)

He didn't get caught. He wasn't wearing a ski mask, just a baseball cap he bought in cash ten minutes before and threw into a dumpster while running away. He stood in the open, right in the alley, with his bright blue eyes beaming, a smile on his lips. He looked pleasant enough. He had gotten dressed in his nice khakis, a button down shirt, and stuck a .38 in his jacket. Then he kissed his mother, and strode out the front door.

He didn't put any bullets in the gun. He didn't have any.

But he knew that a gun in his hand, secretly empty, would get him some cash. Then he planned to get his date a little drunk, and take her to the park, away from the sidewalks and the car headlights. Alone.

And he thought that would be that, that it would all be over, ended.

The first time ended up being his only time, although for years afterwards he thought about it and was tempted to try it again at one point in his life, back when he was still Thymothy, but not since he became Thyme.

And after that time, he didn't think about it for a long time, and never even told Maria about it, and he never thought that he would ever run into the people again.

But a decade late, still years before he was Thyme, Thymothy was sitting in a sandwich shop he had ducked into to avoid a rainstorm that had started up when he was out walking. He was sitting slumped over in his booth, occasionally picking up a cooling fry and eating half of it, drinking a sweet tea, thinking to himself that he should have ordered a beer instead.

He's glancing from the bar, to the television attached above the bar, to the front door, watching the storm blow by. And when he looked over to the tables in the back of the room, near the kitchen, he recognized her.

She sat there, eating a salad and smiling and speaking to a man at the table with her, who had his back to Thymothy.

She ate and listened and then smiled and spoke and ate again.

Thymothy ate some fries.

She stopped eating and looked for her napkin, which she had inadvertently dropped, and she looked his direction. She looked right at him. And she was smiling before she saw him, then made eye contact with him, quit smiling at him, but then smiled again and looked away.

Thymothy was done with his fries. He drank his tea and got up to leave and he looked back one more time and the woman at the table was getting up to leave as well, putting her wallet back into her bag and getting sunglasses out (the storm had blown over quickly) and she rose from her table, leaving her tablemate sitting there still, still facing away from Thymothy.

To in the front door, out, and towards the left, and then take a quick left down the next alley, and he keeps on walking, and then he hits a street and hangs a right on the sidewalk and then crosses over an intersection and turns down one more alley and then catches his breath and starts walking a little slower, and then he finally just starts to head home walking through the alley ways that he's known for so long.

She's nowhere to be seen.

He's stopped looking back, he's just heading home. He looks up, and sees more gray clouds blowing in; he feels the temperature drops a little. After a few minutes raindrops are coming down; the large drop, where it seemed he could step around them as they fell from the sky, but when they hit it was a tiny water bomb. He sped up his steps; and he was watching the wet gravel when he took a quick right from the alley out into the alley and found himself knocking into her, the woman, and he was so startled that he, Thymothy actually fell to the ground, and when she offered him a hand to help him get up, he accepted. And he stood up, and he didn't know what to say, the rain was falling harder now, but he said, "Thanks," and then he wiped some rain off of his face, and he said, "And sorry."

His shirt was wet.

She hadn't said anything to him at all by this point. She nodded, and smiled, and turned to leave, and he said, "Here," reaching into his pocket and pulling out some crumpled bills, and he held them out to her, and he looked at her in the eyes and the bills were getting wet, and she looked at him, and took the bills, and said, "I need an umbrella," and she looked at him, and nodded, and then turned and headed the other direction, and Thymothy watched he as she passed an alcove to a store, where a homeless man was seeking shelter from the rain, and she stopped and handed him the money, and walked off, never looking back at Thymothy, and he turned and walked slowly through the rain.

And, again, he didn't think too much about her, and he didn't see her again for a number of years more.

That wouldn't be the last time he saw her, but it would be the last time that he saw her when he was Thymothy. The next time he saw her was in the grocery store when he was doing Momma's shopping; the next time that Thyme saw Erin, it was while she was on shift managing the local grocery store and Thyme walked in, barefoot and scatterbrained, and Erin saw him, made eye contact, looked down and saw that he had no shoes on, and nodded to him, and then walked away, and he didn't see her again that time.

He came back a few days later, barefoot of course, and smiled to her, and that's when she called him over, and he was afraid that was going to call the police on him, or tell him not to come back, but she looked at him and said, with a blank expression, "They say shoes should be worn in here." She pauses; he nods, she continues, "But I guess I don't care." And that's when Thyme picked up the piece of paper and wrote his statement about taking responsibility for his own feet, and that appeased Erin, and Thyme continued to shop, and they never spoke a word about Thymothy pulling an unloaded gun on Erin and a former boyfriend.

Three decades ago from now, give or take a couple of years, Thymothy's first word was 'bare'. Suzanne thought he was asking for his stuffed bear, until the second word that he uttered, clearly, was 'foot'.

Barefoot.

Thymothy's driver's license was spelled incorrectly for five years; half of his high school year book photos have his name as 'Timothy', a spelling he loathed: "It just isn't me, I'm T-h-y-m-o-t-h-y: Timothy and Thymothy are completely different people."

Momma would say: "If someone can't get your name right, how can you expect them to take the time to build a friendship, or a relationship? They'll just end up hurting you."

The first time Thymothy ever hurt anyone, seriously, it was with a gun and it was a head injury. Suzanne kept a .38 in the house for years, even when the children were young, and they all knew where it was.

The first time he ever hurt a man he was almost thirteen, and had been asleep in his bed. He awoke from sounds from down the hall. He was groggy, confused, his mother was gone and the older kids were his sitter for two nights. Thymothy walked towards Missi's bedroom, and he heard her sounding like she was having trouble breathing. He worried she was in pain. Then he heard a man's voice in there.

He walked barefoot down the hall to Suzanne's room, and grabbed her gun. He cracked Missi's door a little, smelled what he would later know was incense and a dying joint, and peered into the dimly lit room.

A man was on top of his sister, on her bed, naked. He must have been hurting her; she was biting her lips, moaning. Thymothy had heard about rape, and this must be it.

He opened the door and silently ran towards the bed to rescue Mississippi, who was so involved that she didn't see him come into the room. Thymothy sprang up on the mattress and hit the man in the back of the head with the butt of the gun. The man passed out, bleeding, still inside of Missi. Naked, she called an ambulance; young Thymothy, in the meantime, had run back down to his bedroom and hidden himself in the closet not sure if he had saved his sister or killed someone, or both, or neither. He stayed in the closet until the ambulance came to the house and Missi, dressed by then, jumped in the back of the ambulance too and rode to the hospital. Thymothy sat in the back corner of his dark closet for what seemed like a long time, but was maybe twenty minutes, and when he was sure the house was empty and the coast was clear, he put on a sweatshirt, grabbed his sleeping bag and went to the kitchen, where he grabbed a gallon of milk and headed out the back door.

He was in the yard with only the moon lighting the way, and he stood there for a while and finally headed over to the garden shed, where Suzanne kept her plant pots and the lawnmower. Thymothy pulled the lawnmower to block the door, and climbed in over it, and since he didn't know where any flashlights were inside the house, he felt he way into the dark shed, tossed the sleeping bag into a pile, and laid down. Weary of snakes, and spiders, he listened for any movement in the dank shed, and after hearing nothing after a minute or two, he took a big gulp of milk, screwed the top back on, and lay down to sleep on the floor of the shed, hugging the milk carton.

Suzanne came home later and looked into Thyme's room and saw that he was not there. Not concerned yet, she went to look into Missi's room, where she saw some bloody towels on the floor and some blood on the sheets, from the bleeding boyfriend.

Having no idea what was going on, and where Thymothy or Missi were, Suzanne called the police, afraid someone had broken into the house.

The police came with lights blaring, and searched all through the house, and came back into the yard with flash lights, and glanced into the shed, but didn't see the boy sleeping on the floor, hugging the milk container contently.

Soon after a terrified Suzanne leaves with the police to go file a missing child report, Missi and her wounded boyfriend arrive back at the house, unaware that Suzanne has come and gone, and unaware that Thymothy has hidden himself in the back yard. To ease the pain of her boyfriend's head wound, she rolls a joint, and they sit in the front room of the house smoking it. When there's a knock on the front door, Missi, stoned and tired, just jumps up and opens the door, with the joint still smoking in her hand and smoke drifting out of her nose, to find two police officers at the door, late coming to check up on the call that Suzanne made earlier.

The police simply arrest Missi and her boyfriend and take them out and put them in the back of the car, and that's when Suzanne pulled up in the driveway. She sees Missi in the back of the car and pleads with the officers and explains the situation, but the officers see no situation here, and they decide to arrest Missi and her boyfriend and drive off to book them.

Suzanne follows them to the precinct to try to bail them out; the whole time still unaware where Thymothy is.

It's morning before Suzanne gets back to the house with Missi, and they are in the kitchen listening to the morning news on the radio and the news talks about Thymothy, about how there is a missing child, and Suzanne, finally home and concerned and scared, starts to cry, and Missi hugs her, and that's when Thymothy walked back into the house, dragging his sleeping bag behind him and the half-empty carton of milk held under his arm.

Years later, they would sit in the kitchen, Missi and her brother, smoking a joint while Suzanne was out on a date and laugh about the time that Thymothy busted open her boyfriend's skull, they would laugh about that for years, especially after that same boyfriend cheated on her with a friend, and they laughed about it until Missi took her fatal swim in that river. (Nasty currents.)

Chapter Seven

Photojournalism, Exercise, and Other Forms of Suicide

Now it's now, and it's dusk, on a Tuesday night:

He isn't working tonight.

It's a little chilly, as a late September evening can be, but his beard keeps his face warm. The warmth from a beard wasn't recognizable to Thyme until he grew a beard, shaved it, and then grew it back again. He likes a beard; never a moustache or a goatee. His comes in the color of a nice lager in a mug. He recently cut his hair; it was a little shaggy; Momma called it unruly. So he cut it.

Now it's dusk, two days past a haircut.

He's bare foot and walking, singing folk songs he'd heard on NPR Sunday afternoon. He's got some film in his camera. Black and white. He's happy he can still find some decent .35 millimeter film with all the digital cameras around. Thyme likes his .35 millimeter cameras.

There's a detachable camera flash in the other pocket.

He walks a lot in the neighborhood around Suzanne's house, and each walk has a larger radius.

He pulls the flash out of his pocket.

When he turns it on, there's always an audible surge of the battery, lasting maybe a second. He loved that sound as a child. Still does, too.

He walks around the neighborhood; it's getting darker now but it's not too late, it's fall and he has to take his walks earlier as the days get shorter.

Thyme raises his camera to his eye, focuses it on one nearby house, and snaps a shot, then he repeats and shoots the house next to that one, then the one across the street, and one to the right of that one and then to the right of that one. He walks on, five minutes, six, humming to himself, thinking about how he cut his hair too short, how many canned yams he'd have to start shelving for the upcoming holiday season. He stops, raises his camera, and continues with the random shots, taking pictures of what surrounds him.

These houses all seem empty to him. There are no cars in the driveways for five or six of them, ones in a square. People should be home, he thought, it's late enough in the evening. No kitchen lights are on; no porch lights are on. Thyme sees it is almost a whole block of houses for sale, vacant, victims of the housing bubble burst and foreclosure boom, the recession confusion, the stock market correction, the unemployment generation. But there is one house lit up, right in the center of empties; there is one house with the kitchen lights on, a bathroom light on, a flickering television downstairs.

Thyme walks across the street and sits in the yard of a vacant house, a colonial with a blue porch and a lawn that needs weeding and raking. He sits for a few minutes, he thinks about the pot plant in the backyard, budding, he thinks about the tits of the woman he saw jogging a little while ago. He sees an empty pack of cigarettes next to the curb and his fingers and tongue gets a mind of their own, he can taste them, eyes looking for a full pack on the ground. "No, no," he says through his beard, "we've stopped that junk too."

He sits cross legged; the house behind him sits empty, and the house across from him is bright but with no signs of movement. A car in the driveway sits facing the closed garage door; it's a light blue 4-door sedan, a Toyota, maybe four or five years old, he thinks. He sees where one bumper sticker has been removed from the left part of the fender leaving rectangular gray residue; on the right side is a yin and yang symbol on a round sticker. Black and white.

He stares at the back of that car, the car almost matching his eyes. His red white and blue eyes stare at the car that appears to have the blues in all ways.

It reminds him of a car that Maria used to have. He's lost in himself a little bit, staring at the blue car. He looks at the stickers, one here, one gone. He tries to imagine what the other one once said.

He can see the lights in the house, but he can't hear the television.

He sits and closes his eyes, resting for a moment. He'll get up and go home in a minute, fix some hot tea, watch the war channel, the infidel channel, the suffering channel. But for now, he rests his eyes; he closes them, and they stay shut.

Pop!
Whoa! What?
He's awake.

He's confused; what just happened, what was that? His camera hangs from neck; his hair is still two days after a cut on a barefoot skinny skeleton. His feet are still there, calloused. But that was a shot.

Yes. He heard a shot. And nearby, too.

But there was something else.

Some movement. Something falling. A thud. A cracking noise.

The lights from the double paned, curtained windows spill out into the yard across the street from him, the brick sideway, the driveway.

There's a body. Thyme can see it now. He knows it wasn't there a minute ago, but there's a body there and it's dead, he knows. Right in front of the car, on the asphalt driveway, between the car and garage. And it's a dead body, Thyme can see that. Dead now, at least.

He hasn't moved yet, not much at least. He'd held his breathe for a second or two; you never know what's going on in the world these days, he wasn't about to hop up and run over.

Thyme lifts the camera to his eye and snaps a few frames. He's a photojournalist now, he feels, here in suburbia, he's capturing something unique. You're a photojournalist, he tells himself. Take the pictures. Take pictures. Quickly.

It's almost dark now. All the empty houses sit still, lifeless. A skull bleeds onto cracked black asphalt. He takes two photos of the house and of the blue car and starts to walk away.

"Momma, it's weird, but when I was sitting there, well I was into my own thoughts but I had a feeling that someone was there, but then I forgot about it. He must have been sitting up there on the roof when I came and sat across the street. Maybe, this is weird, but he was maybe waiting for me to leave, before he shot himself."

"Maybe he didn't know you were there, sitting in front of him," she's putting on lipstick.

What Thyme didn't see, however, is that there's still a woman on the roof, crouched next to a dormer window, head upon her knees, sitting in the cool evening air, crying silently.

It's not her house; she only recently started living there, and she never meant to live there, but she had to move somewhere.

That is her car though, the blue one in the drive way, the one that's just inches away from the blood stains. She's the one who put the stickers on the bumper; she's the one who took one of them off.

Thyme never noticed her up there, he just looked down on the driveway, took his photos, and walked away.

What he doesn't see later is the blue police lights, red ambulance lights, sirens on and then off, loud two-way radios, men with moustaches and badges, and a woman saying "It's over, you're alright, Chastity."

Chapter Eight

An Erratic History of Thyme, Part Four

Thyme thought he was always running out of it, time that is. He often felt that the hours and seconds were cruising through his fingers in front of his blue eyes. He thought that with time his eyes might change color. "Sometimes kids are born with blond hair and it turns brown, maybe my eyes will turn brown."

Suzanne Exler smiles and flips through a remodeling magazine, patient for her tea that's steeping in her mug, within reach.

"Or green," he'd say, not wanting her to think he didn't like the color of her eyes.

"They're just fine as they are, son. You're fine as you are." That was when Thyme felt like he had no time and he was Thymothy. Now, he's Thyme and time's all he's got.

It seems to Thyme that the majority of the conversations he's had with Momma in the past, oh say, twenty years have taken place at this table, on the same chairs which get new stains and then reupholstered every five years. And, if not here, they're in her car, driving around too fast, talking slowly.

Maybe she got that mug over there, the one in the sink, when Thyme was in high school, the high school that he now still lives within walking distance from. His guidance counselor was a man then in his fifties with an olive complexion, one front tooth, and a beer belly. In a paisley tie he'd sigh heavily and say, "Mist-er h-Exler, you're, uh, you're not working up to, uh, your potential."

Thymothy raised an eyebrow; a slight shrug.

"You haven't turned in your physics homework in three weeks, do you realize that? Three weeks."

"Okay."

"What do you plan to do next year? Community college?" He wipes his forehead and sighs, "The military perhaps?"

"No, no military; no more school either. I'm in no hurry to go anywhere."

Thyme, then Thymothy, made some money working at a restaurant for a while after graduation and after a year or so he bought a camera and some tools (a table saw, a hammer), and he quit the restaurant, and started working in carpentry, working for a neighbor.

But he always wanted to be a photographer.

Even now, years later, as he's back living with Momma a decade and a half after he graduated from high school, he'll turn on the television and see pictures of a big earthquake, of burning poppy fields, burning embassies, and mention about how he wanted to be there, taking those photos.

"Photojournalism is just employment," Suzanne lectured her son two days ago at the kitchen table, "and it's suicide." She's always sipping tea. "Avoid it. Employment. And suicide."

NPR voices are speaking in relaxed voices about levees bursting and oil pipelines being bombed, hurricanes: Cuba flooded, Jamaica somehow spared the day before; the Mexican army is being kidnapped by drug cartel's thugs, as the rain rapes and the wind ravages.

Thyme is thinking about his camera. The lens. The flash.

Later that afternoon, Thyme is in the kitchen, smoking a joint, and cutting carrots for a salad Momma is making, and he slices his hand. The blood falls onto the orange carrots, staining them red. Thyme picks up the stained pieces, washes the blood off, holds his bleeding hand under the cold running water, and he chomps into some of the carrots, a taste of blood mixes with the sweetness of the small carrots. The water keeps on running; he keeps munching carrots.

With his other hand, the one that's not bleeding, he turns off the water, and then picks up a semi-clean wash rag, and holds it against the open cut, and he walks outside, thinking about smoking, tasting blood-dripped carrots on his tongue.

He walks to the back door, opens it, leaves it ajar, and sits on the back steps, staring out into the yard, daydreaming. His eyes are wide; his wound is throbbing; his head hurts; he wishes he was tired. But he's not. His hand feels swollen, but is not. He can feel his pulse in the cut.

He walks around to the front of the house, and sits on the concrete steps watching the traffic. Cars are parked along the side of the road; he wishes he had one. As he watches, a large black bird comes down and lands on the closest car, still fifteen or twenty feet from where Thyme is sitting. The bird freezes from motion, and sits on the car perfectly still, and Thyme thinks he can hear the bird growling at him: a deep, guttural sound like a didgeridoo played in a dank cave.

The bird stares and stares, and Thyme stares back; forgetting about the throbbing in his fingers. After a few minutes, Thyme gets up and runs towards the bird, who doesn't move, but stares and growls some more, apparently unaffected by Thyme's approach.

Thyme barks towards the growling bird, getting no response.

Thyme sneezes; the bird yawns, growling the whole duration of the yawn, and when the yawn is over, the bird stretches out his wings, cocks his head, and takes flight, aiming directly at Thyme.

The bird gets uncomfortably close to Thyme, and Thyme momentarily forgets about the wounded hand, and he holds both hands up in front of his face, to deflect this winged adversary. When the bird gets close, it stops its devilish growl, and grips the blood-soaked dishrag, and pulls it away from Thyme, and caws once, from deep in its throat, and then flies away, above the sidewalk, dripping little blood patterns onto the asphalt below, and Thyme runs behind for a little bit, he too dripping blood. As he walks back to his house, he follows a trail of blood, and finds himself looking over his shoulder for that massive black bird's return.

But it never does.

And each time that Thyme goes out for his walk, his bare feet step on his dried blood. He's walking the next day, and he scrapes his toe, and bends down to make sure that his toe nail is still attached (it is), and a black feather falls from the sky above him; but by the time he's picked up the feather and decided his toe nail wasn't going to fall off (today), he looks up into the sky, and he cannot see any birds at all, he doesn't hear any birds calling or singing, and certainly not one growling at him.

"Momma?"

"Yes, Thyme?"

"I think a bird is out to get me."

"Thyme, I . . ."

"I know what you're gonna say, Momma: 'There are things I don't understand about this world yet', or something like that."

Momma looks back down at the paper in front of her and goes back to sipping on her tea and say, "No, actually."

"No what?"

"No, I wasn't going to say that."

She's silent; offers no more conversation.

After a minute, Thyme asks, "What were you going to say."

She puts her tea down, closes the paper and says, "It's a two-parter. An either-or."

"What is Momma?"

"My response."

"And, that is what?"

"Well, first, I'd say that you smoke too much pot."

"Fair enough. And second?"

"Second, I'd stay away from that bird, if I were you."

"Momma?"

"Yes, Thyme?"

"Do you think that was a painkiller ghost?"

"I'm not sure that was a ghost."

"But if it was; it didn't seem normal."

"Did it make you feel better?"

"No."

"Well, then, there you go." She raises an eyebrow and smiles for a second, and then breaks eye contact and stares out the window. She looks back at the table for a second and then she takes the final sip from her tea, smiles, gets up, her cell phone and a paperback book from the counter, waves, and walks away.

Thyme hears her car start; he looks out the window, expecting to see the black bird peering back at him, growling.

But doesn't.

Chapter Nine

A Homemade Darkroom and
a Man's Dead Best Friend

Thyme develops those pictures.

They show a man face down on the asphalt, very dead. In the corner of the photo is that bumper sticker of the yin and the yang on the blue car.

The film is black and white. So the car is gray. The blood is black.

The photos show something he didn't see when he took them. In the top corner, on the roof near a dormer window is something that looks just a little out of focus. He enlarges the image. It's a little grainy, but it's a person: hunched over, leaning against the side of the dormer.

The next day, he pulls on a sweatshirt, drinks a cup of hot tea and leaves for his walk. He's going back there, to that house. It's a little later in the evening then the last time he walked there so it's a little darker; Thyme loves this time of year.

When he gets there, everything is the same. The For Sale signs are still in the yards. Price Reduced. Bank Short Sale. Foreclosure. But the house that he came to look at is dark now, too. The blue car is still there, in the exact same space that it was a day or two ago, its yin and yang to the right, the remains of a missing sticker to the left. The front door is closed, and the television is off.

He looks up at the roof, the empty roof. He takes three photos. He keeps looking at the house, the roof, the black trash bags peeping out of the topless trash can in the side yard. The windows were dark, the trees are lonely, some dropping leaves, some still green and yellow.

He shoulders his camera and turns and walks home, to the walk-in closet in the spare bedroom, Missi's old room, to develop more shots.

The woman on the roof is named Chastity.

She wasn't on the roof now. Thyme had been looking for her in a vague way. She was inside the dark house now, on the sofa, losing weight from not eating, humming lullabies to the emptiness, crying to the wallpaper, talking to the television.

Thyme had also been hoping to see that man, that dead man alive, gone but here, like a scratch on a negative, always there, but never here.

He was hoping to see that man, alive and well, sitting on the roof, next to the dormer, but he didn't; but Thyme fears that the man is gone, but not yet in the ground, in that limbo between where he was and where he will never leave. Thyme looks at the photos, waiting for something to change, waiting for the body to move a finger, a muscle, but it never does.

He stares, when he walks to that house at night, he stares to where the body fell, where it just seemed to drop from the clouds. He imagines watching it unhappen, reverse itself, the skull uncracking, the teeth unbreaking, the drops of blood raining upwards, the body lifting up from the driveway, and flying upwards from the ground, landing on the roof, in a quiet, crouching position, and then the backwards pop of a gun, and the small cloud of smoke jumping into the barrel. But he never sees this; he never sees an image of that man at all.

But he's walking home and he hears a bark, slightly familiar, and then he smells a dog, he smells his old dog, the one that lived with him when he was Thymothy, the one that used to stare at him and Maria until they fed him their own food; he hears those familiar tags on the collar, and hears panting, but he never sees a dog. But the whole way home, he feels like he's being followed, the tags always sound nearby, so he takes a picture of the empty sidewalk behind him.

And when he develops the photo of the empty sidewalk, he sees a blur at the bottom, a blur about the size and shape of a dog, like the one that used to follow him everywhere, but that was years ago.

Chapter Ten

Popping Pain Pills for Breakfast, Again

Camera slung over his shoulder, Thyme walks out the door, barefoot, and right on the heels of Suzanne, who's off to meet a man for brunch. He waves goodbye. She sits in her car, turns it on; he scratches his beard, pulls the baseball cap down a little more.

It's earlier in the day than he normally starts, so he can take a longer walk. He's walking a little farther to a park. He likes to go there with his camera and his bare feet poking out of tan corduroys. He's been coming here since he was a child. It's not for the nature; he likes to stumble upon people, situations, and give the camera a shot or two. Situations in the city: a couple making out next to the lake, people arguing on the tennis courts, young kids passing joints next to their skateboards, a woman reading a Bible on a bench, trees changing color above kids arguing over a soccer match, brown bags with beer cans left under magnolia trees, a homeless man on the corner asking for change.

He's in the park now. The grounds keeper knows him by sight, not necessarily by name.

"Hul-lo Shutterbug."

"Hello, Caretaker."

He's strolling through the grass, occasionally lifting the camera to his eye. He focuses on some birds looking for seeds. There is a woman sitting under a willow, weeping, and Thyme turns the lens towards her for three snaps of the shutter. He isn't close enough to hear her cry, but he can see her shoulders shaking. He takes another photo of her.

She's about his age, he guesses, with pretty brown hair, past her shoulders. She's slight, slender even.

She doesn't notice him taking pictures.

But she didn't notice a few nights ago, either, when he took pictures of her on the roof.

He's taken about a half dozen photos of her and he slings the camera strap over one shoulder, pulls the lens cap from his back pocket and puts it in its place.

She never knows that he was there; doesn't know that he's been within 50 yards of her three times in the past week. This is the first time that Thyme has ever actually seen her, been able to focus on her.

But he doesn't know who she is.

And he doesn't wonder what her name is; he doesn't wonder why she's crying. He's not wondering about who she is or where she's from; he's wondering how the photos are going to come out, hoping they're in focus. He's not paying attention to the blue bag lying on the ground next to her ankles.

He's not wondering about what's in that knitted blue bag.

He turns and keeps on walking.

Pop! He's shot!

He's hit! The camera falls and crashes to the ground; the lens cap pops off. He is shocked, stumbles down on the cement sidewalk; the grounds keeper sees and is running towards Thyme.

A bullet cracks a bone.

Blood spills.

He's on the ground, confused and bleeding, and his arm feels like it's been smashed, set on fire, and he knows he's been shot because he's been shot before; it burns!

The grounds keeper is talking quickly into a cell phone, saying, "I'm getting someone Shutterbug!" Some people are running away, a couple of people are coming towards Thyme to help. Thyme's bleeding, feeling like he's on fire. Again. He's been shot in the left arm this time, low, in the wrist.

His focusing hand.

Later that day, he wakes up with bandages on his left wrist in a hospital bed. Suzanne is sitting in a chair by the window reading a mystery novel she bought in the hospital gift shop. He squints at her; she smiles at him, dog-ears the page and sets the book on the floor.

He looks at his bandaged wrist, it's shattered. He feels a little sick. He can't feel any of his fingers.

There's an I.V. going into his arm, dripping, and his stomach feels warm; he feels that familiar warmth, right before the itching starts, leading into those dreamy dazes.

What does Suzanne know that Thyme doesn't know?

Just a little: that he's lost most of the control of his hand, at least for a while, physical therapy awaits him; the camera is bashed and broken, but it's sitting here in the hospital room, under her chair.

Bones are shattered; tendons slashed and stitched, skinned burnt. His eyelids are getting heavy again and Suzanne picks up her book, open her pages, and his eyes shut.

Drip drip, drowsy.

Dream drip, dream.

He hears the tags of his dog, the one that died years ago, following him down the sidewalk, imageless.

Drip, drip.

Dream.

Part Two

Shooting You Is the Closest I'll Get to Sleeping With You, No Name, & Other Feel Goods

Chapter Eleven

I'm a Little Annie, I'm a Little Annie

"I'm a little Annie, I'm a little Annie."

That's what Chastity would always say, since she was a child, through now, when she's thirty. "I'm a little Annie now, tomorrow, and always have been."

This is what she means: she always leaves out the word 'orphan'.

This is who she is: little orphan Chastity.

She's always known she was an orphan; but she's not like little orphan Annie. She doesn't have red hair, doesn't so much trust stray dogs, and never has been one for musicals. She spent time in an orphanage, lived in a few foster homes, and never had any of those television talk show horrors: no abuse; all of the homes clothed her and fed her, but she always felt alone, always alone in the middle of things.

This is what she is: a virgin.

This is what she says: "I'm a little Annie: she never screwed around and neither do I. Besides, there are too many kids in the world; I don't want to chance making another. I'm happy not having any relatives, any blood relatives. I'm happy being an orphan."

Chastity's a little Annie.

That's how she is now, that's how she has been, and that's how she wants to remain, a little Annie. Orphan. She's Orphan Annie, without the dog and without the songs and without the rich bald foster dad, although having more than just a few pennies in the bank would be nice.

What was in that blue bag that day Thyme saw her crying in the park? Thyme had noticed it, but he didn't think too much of it. Now he's figured it out.

Now he's skipping cereal and he's popping pain pills for breakfast, again.

He knows what to do: he swallows the first one whole and chews up the next one. Eat breakfast and repeat.

This is nothing new.

The gun that shot Thyme, this time, was in Chastity's blue bag. She'd never seen him before. She had never seen him until she looked up and there he was on the sidewalk, camera bouncing lens down, his knees buckling, blood on the sidewalk.

She had the gun to shoot herself.

She had picked it up, out of the bag, the blue one. But she wasn't ready to shoot herself; it wasn't even aimed towards her. But it went off.

It just went off, she thought the safety was on; she wasn't ready to use it yet. She was still just thinking about it.

But it went off and it scared the breath out of her. Her red eyes saw blue smoke. She saw the man she shot. She saw his knees shaking.

And she had shot him.

She got up, unnoticed, and walked through the trees away from Thyme, and headed towards the pond. (If he was looking at her now, he'd see she was just a little shorter than he is.) At the edge of the pond, she threw the gun in; she stuffed her blue bag in a metal trash bin down the path. She started to run.

Thyme was on the ground, moaning and bleeding, his camera ruined, film exposed, he was in shock.

She ran.

Thyme was taken to the hospital. He was in and out of consciousness; he heard the sirens of the ambulance; he smelled his old dog, the one that died years ago. He knows that smell. The wet fur smell after the dog had jumped into the pond and swam; he felt the invisible tongue licking his cheek before he closed his eyes for a minute, and woke up after being placed on a stretcher and taken to the ambulance; when the doors shut, he heard a faint whimper and that jingle again.

Chapter Twelve

Indecent Exposure, Masturbation, and No Rape

Chastity had shot two men before; Thyme was her third victim.

The first man that she shot, she shot in the groin.

She had been walking home (not too far from Main and Meadow), and a man, drunk or cracked up, came out of an alley towards her with a broken bottle in his left hand and his right hand holding himself and urinating at her, shouting "I'm gonna eat you, girl! I'm gonna cook you, girl! Girl!" And he leaped at her, urinating on her foot, and he swung the broken bottle at her, snagging the fabric of her coat, but not ripping through, and he spit and gritted his teeth and said, "I'm gonna chew you and smoke you, Ashley! I'm gonna cut you, Susan! Girl! Girl!"

And he let go of himself and took hold of his broken bottle like it was a baseball bat and he licked his lips and yelled, with spit flying everywhere, "You're going to die, Sara! But I'm going to screw you first, Megan!"

And Chastity took a step backwards and kicked her boots at him as he was swinging and he shouted "Girl! I'm going to sleep with you for eternity, girl!"

Chastity stuck her hand into her coat pocket.

She grasped her small revolver in her coat pocket, struggled to get it out, hardly aimed, and shot the man right in the groin and then yelled "Shooting you is the closest I'll get to sleeping with you!"

And then she took off running.

Running, and running, and running.

("I've always been sort of a freak magnet.")

Now, after shooting Thyme, Chastity was taken to the hospital.

After she was found by a groundskeeper, hysterical in the bushes, smelling like pine needles, ivy, and gun powder, she was taken to the same hospital that Thyme was.

She had run into the woods after hiding the gun and passed out in some bushes, exhaustion with her skirt nearly torn off by thorns and branches, crying quietly. She was crying and shaking, feeling alive but wanting to die. Her make-up was running down her cheek; her legs were bleeding a little from the bushes.

"I think we've got a rape here!" She hears footsteps on the leaves near her; more voices.

She looked as if she had been assaulted: left hand down the front of her skirt, crying, tears running mascara down her cheeks, taking heavy sighs, blood from thorn scrapes running down her legs, into her shoes.

The grounds keeper, the one that Thyme knows by sight but not by name, came up, already punching numbers into his cell phone. "I think we've got a rape here!"

It seemed to take a long time for a second ambulance to come (one was called for the gunshot victim, too), with strangers running up to help, her cheeks were scratched and exposed, 'Rape' being yelled and here's Chastity crying, her fingers jammed down her rarely worn panties into her pubic hair (which now smells like a handgun), and she's shot a stranger, and she's repeating in a hushed voice: "No, no, I'm a virgin, no, please, please leave me alone, please."

"We got a rape here!"

"No, no, please, I'm a virgin, please leave me."

Exhausted, her eyes close. (Dreams of warmth.)

She awoke in a hospital. (Cold chills.)

It was strange to wake up in a hospital, alive, no rape, no suicide, cuts maybe but nothing more. She remembers the shot, the sickening thud of a skull breaking, bits of brains near her front tire; she remembers walking in the driveway two days later, the body was gone, but she found a tooth on the driveway, a molar, cracked and bloody.

She thought how strange it was to be waking up in a hospital, alive, no assault, just another man shot right there, right in front of her. She can't understand what's happened all of a sudden; not just now, or today, but recently.

She spited herself: Why couldn't she just have shot herself?

She asked herself: Why didn't she just go to the other side of the tree, take the gun out of the bag, put it up touching the roof of her mouth, and pull the trigger? She thought about putting the mouth of the gun into her left ear, pointing a little up, but not too far. Or just to her temple. If she had only put that gun right between her eyebrows, right under where the wrinkles will form in fifteen years, she could have put it there and pulled the trigger and when the bullet cracked through the rear of her skull it would be lodged in the tree trunk and no one else would have gotten hurt.

But here she was, in a hospital gown that felt like indecent exposure, no hole in her head, no hole in her ear, no hole in her mouth, no bullet lodged in the oak tree behind her non-penetrated skull. But there was someone else shot; she could have killed him, might have shot off a dick again, she didn't know.

She's in a hospital gown, a virgin, not expecting to be alive today; the nurses are looking at her like she's a druggie from up in the Hill. But she's not. She's never snorted or injected anything, throws up from more than one pain pill, and hates having a hangover so much she rarely drinks.

But she lies down on the bed after the nurses leave, and thinks about indecent exposure, accidental shootings, and no rape. And it feels good then to be thinking about these things; it feels good to be on the bed, in the dark, in the quiet room, thinking about whatever, just whatever she wanted to.

Chapter Thirteen

Shooting You Is the Closest
I'll Get to Sleeping With You

The hospital staff kept her overnight for evaluation.

She was allowed to watch TV, go to the cafeteria, or wander the halls, do just about anything, except leave. She hadn't eaten much recently; they fed her. She heard the nurses talking about a man getting shot in the arm at the park, and that he was here in this hospital. 'It must be him,' she knew. And she figured out which floor he was on, there weren't many and she could rule out the pediatric ward and the woman's pavilion and ruled out the ER and ICU (she didn't shoot anyone in the groin, not this time).

She followed nurses; she listened in on their conversations. She peered in through the door to look at him, asleep in his bed, the television turned to the news, photojournalists kidnapped in Gaza, fighters killed in Lebanon; child kidnappings in Florida. He was asleep in her bed; snoring slightly in a painkiller dream.

There had been a woman in his room, Chastity noticed, an older woman, his mother of course. And she thought to herself: here she was, she had shot this woman's son. But the woman left and Chastity walked into the room, like she was supposed to be there. She went to the bed, and she looked down on to his meal tray and saw his name on the food order: here, passed out on pain pills and hospital macaroni and cheese, was 'Thymothy X Exler'.

As she is standing there, hovering over him like a guardian angel, he opens his eyes and looks around the room. She can tell by his woozy movements that he is about to close his eyes again and he blinks a few times and closes his eyes. She was able to see his eyes, his blue eyes.

She left the room wondering what the X stood for.

She walked down the hall thinking to herself, "I shot Baby Blue Eyes. I shot Baby Blue Eyes. I shot Baby Blue Eyes."

Later, Chastity waited until Thyme's mother had left again and she snuck back into his room. He was asleep again.

His beard looked dirty and she thought that his hair should be a little longer.

Chastity stood over him for a little bit, looked at his bandaged hand, she touched his beard just a little bit, snagged a little by accident, and there was no way for her to know that he was dreaming of Maria touching his beard just now, just like years ago.

It's been years and he's still dreaming of her. ("Maybe it's because you have no one else to dream of," Suzanne once told her son. "I don't really want to dream of anyone else, Momma, but I also don't want to dream of her.")

Chastity backed away, sat down on the chair that Momma Exler had been sitting on all day, and she wiped her eyes, scratched her nose, and said "Shooting you was an accident," staring at the closed eyes of sleeping Thyme. "I bet shooting you is the closest I'll get to sleeping with you, too." There were tears in her eyes.

She spotted the busted camera under the chair that she had been sitting in, and she leaned over and picked it up.

She held the camera and said to herself, 'I'm a virgin, not an angel.'

She left the room, picking up a blanket and stealing the broken camera hidden within it.

Thyme woke up not too long after Chastity had taken his camera.

Suzanne was in the chair, texting on her cell phone.

"I had a dream, Momma, a dream about Maria. She was touching me, my beard, and it was so real. It's like I could feel her, smell her, hear her sitting right there, talking to me."

Suzanne, stroking his cheek and holding his good hand, said, "Oh, that was just me. I've been right here, reading, touching you on the face now and again."

It wasn't until Thyme was going home that Suzanne realized the camera was gone. She asked the nurses if they had seen it, moved it, or noticed it, but no one had.

But now we're back to Chastity, a little while ago, before they left the hospital:

"Shooting you is the closest I'll get to sleeping with you."

But this time she was speaking to Thyme. But the way that she said it today and the way she said it a few years ago were different.

("I'm a virgin, not an angel!")

But today she was saying it with sorrow, as an apology. An apology to a man she didn't know, who couldn't hear her, and who she never meant to shoot.

She'd never been shot before, but now she's shot her third victim, saying to each of them 'Shooting you is the closest I'll get to sleeping with you.' And now Thyme's been shot for a second time; he's never shot anyone before, though of course he's aimed a gun at people before.

His left hand will be out of commission for a while ("I'll just have to get a lighter camera, Momma.").

And a few days before, with the man on the roof, as Chastity hid under her hair near the dormers, before the man on the roof shot himself in the left eye, while the eyes were open and staring at Chastity, right before he pulled the trigger he spit on the shingles and said, "I guess shooting myself is the closest I'll get to sleeping with you."

And then he was no more.

("I'm a virgin, not an angel.")

He's an angel now, not a virgin.

Bang bang.

Dreamless, now.

Chapter Fourteen

the Hiding Girl

This is now, about a week ago: she's hiding.

She's hiding beneath cushions and pillows from the sofa and she says softly, "I'm a virgin, not an angel."

The pillows fell as she spoke. There is a man, No Name, in the room; he's slightly older than Chastity, drinking bottled water, and leaning against the wall.

And then she says, "And I've always been sort of a freak magnet."

The reply: "I'll say."

No Name, bottle in hand, walks a few steps and then breaks a light bulb by taking a lamp by the base and smashing it headlong into the wall.

He removes his watch and throws his watch to the floor and kicks it to the wall where it slams and stops. He walks over to the fortress of pillows and throws them off of Chastity; he throws them forcefully and recklessly away, one this way at a plate and it falls shattering on the floor, another towards a framed picture, which falls onto the floor. He walks over to the picture, and smashes his bare heel into the glass.

He shuts one eye and opens the other eye wider. He takes a few steps back; a shard of glass is wedged into his heel.

She says, "I'll say."

He says, "I want you so much, but that is the difference between us." He stops for a second, but keeps looking right at her and then gets out, "And I hate that," and he barely says this.

She says, "Just being close to you is the closest I'll get to sleeping with you; unless you want me to shoot you."

She thinks she means the last part like a joke, but she's not sure.

He looks away and walks out of the room, down the hallway past the half bathroom, and up the stairs to the second floor, leaving blood stains wherever his left heel lands.

She follows, down the hall, up the stairs. She walks in the spare bedroom, the 'library' as they call it, with bookshelves packed tight with hardbacks and paperbacks and records and magazines. There's a window in the room, she can feel a breeze and see the red glow of his cigarette and smell the tobacco when he exhales through his nostrils, looking out over the quiet street. All the houses around his are dark; like they were evacuated for some anthrax scare and no one bothered to knock on this door; or like in New Orleans after the hurricane hit, when people lived off propane stoves for months with warm beers for painkillers.

He smokes out the window, looking absently at the dark houses.

Then he crawls through the window, out onto the roof, and sits against the dormer window, smoking his filtered cigarette. She walks across the room, through the lingering smoke, past yellowed paperbacks, encyclopedias, and photo albums; she climbs through the window and carefully maneuvers herself onto the roof near him, but not right next to him, leaning back against the wooden frame of the window.

The neighborhood is completely quiet.

He turns his head towards her and slaps her across the cheek, slaps her hard. He doesn't say a word to her, but then spits at her, and hits her hard in the cheeks with his fist.

He stands up and says to her as she's crying, "I guess me shooting myself is the closest I'll get to sleeping with you."

He has a gun with him; Chastity knew he kept the guns in the library. He aims the revolver at her chest, then raises it and places it against his temple, stares at her, keeps his eyes wide open, he watches the wind blow her hair around, she's crying and a little puffy already from where he slapped her, and then he moves the gun from his temple and pushes it against his left eye and pulls the trigger then falls two stories landing head down on the driveway.

The neighborhood is still and quiet.

Chastity is in tears and paralyzed.

There are no clouds in the sky but she thinks that she sees a few bright, brief flashes of lightning; but they don't seem to be coming from the sky, she's just confused, she tells herself. It's just sheet lighting. It's only lightning, just not up in the sky.

Chapter Fifteen

Higgledy-Piggledy, Little Red Hiding Hood, & van Gogh-to-Hell in the Cornfield

Now it's now, and this is how it is:

Chastity sleeps in a t-shirt on the couch in the living room. She's slept on more sofas than beds in her life. Behind shut windows with closed curtains, she sleeps in a t-shirt and nothing else, a red t-shirt; she's Little Red Hiding Hood on the sofa, in the TV room. Outside the curtained windows, the sun is shining, cars go by, and a leaf blower is blowing on the next block down, where people still appear to live. A random leaf blower wakes her from her nap.

She's wearing a t-shirt, and nothing else, and she's staring at the television: suicide car drivers in Baghdad, explosives strapped to shoppers in Kabul bazaars, night clubs being blown up mid-song in Tel Aviv. Bad spinach kills sixteen in the Midwest. Twelve men found dead three miles outside of Mexico City. All the commercials are for hard-on pills.

It seems the world around her is dying off in violence, religion, sex, and suicides. She figured a few days ago there were two different types of suicides, the kind where you go alone and the kind where you take people with you.

When she was thinking about killing herself, she thought that of the two options, she'd kill herself and no one else. And looked what happened. She had a victim, she shot a man; she just wanted to kill herself, not hurt anyone else.

The first time that she touched herself, there, was about five minutes before the first time she shot a man. The man was chasing her through the woods screaming "Higgledy-piggledy, boo-boo, higgledy-piggledy, ah!" and she responded, "Shooting you is the closest I'll get to sleeping with you!"

Why was Chastity out there in those woods?

It was about a dozen years ago now, which was when she got her first gun. She had made a decision. She decided never to sleep with a man, but she had to know what an orgasm felt like.

She decided it was time.

She decided that she couldn't do it at home; not here in her small bedroom on her hand-me-down mattress with no box springs and the television on in the other room, and the dishwasher running, and a dog barking at the kids playing outside.

So she left.

She went outside and followed a path into some woods that she had walked through once before, and then she branched off from the trail.

She had worn a skirt, shoes, socks, bra, and shirt but had intentionally left her underwear at home. She laid down, looking up between some spaces of the trees at the fluffy clouds, and then closed her eyes for a minute, two, put her hand down her skirt and then she opened her eyes and she saw him coming at her from the bushes. And just as the man tackled her, she screamed and she kicked the man off of her and she got up and ran.

She looked back; the man was following her, shouting "Higgledy-piggledy, boo-boo, higgledy-piggledy, ah!" And she was terrified and he was chasing her, yelling, bending down every now and then to pick up rocks to throw at her, hitting her once on the back of the head and twice in her back.

She ran without looking back, as to avoid a rock hitting her in the face.

She had grabbed her bag as she got up, the bag which had her revolver in it. She ran the opposite direction from where she had come and she wished that she hadn't because she didn't know this part of the woods too well, and shortly she found herself leaving the woods and entering into a corn field. The corn was about ready for harvest, the stalks were up over her head for the most part.

The man is not too tall, about her height, and maybe in his forties, with short hair, a reddish beard and a bandage over one ear. "Higgledy-piggledy, boo-boo, higgledy-piggledy, ah, ah!" His belt was now undone, his brown leather shoes crushing corn stalks as he stumbled after her. One final rock flew by her head.

She yelled for him to back off, to get away. She's lost in the field.

She yelled to back off but he was getting closer, he had almost reached her and then her foot got wrapped in a fallen cornstalk and she lost her pace, he reached her, grabbed her shoulder, but then he lost his footing, too, and stumbled and fell and she got away, for a second.

She looked back again, and with the hair and the beard and the bandage, she thought of Vincent van Gogh chasing her through the cornfield. She ran on, trying to find a way out of the corn.

She managed to get a few steps ahead after he fell and reached into her bag and rumbled around until she had her fist on the handle of the gun and pulled it out and turned to the man and shouted for him to "Get out of here, you freaky van Gogh, van Gogh-to-Hell!" but he kept coming at her, shouting "Higgledy-piggledy, boo-boo, higgledy-piggledy, ah!" and then she aimed and she said "Shooting you is the closest I'll get to sleeping with you!", and she shot him in the stomach, and he fell down screaming, "Boo-boo! Boo-boo! Ah, ah!"

Chastity says, to herself, "I just shot van Gogh, I just shot van Gogh-to-Hell!"

She ran and looked back. She ran after shooting the man, after indecent exposure, masturbation, and no rape. As she ran, she heard in the field, "Ah, ah! Boo-boo!"

She read a blip in the paper two days later that a man was found dead in a field from a gunshot, there were no leads. She closed the Metro section and turned on the news.

("I've always been sort of a freak magnet.")

That was the first time she ever shot a man. That was years ago, before there were ten War Channels, before this war, these wars, those wars, when the main news was debate over if the President had inhaled or had too much fun in the oval office.

Chastity thinks about indecent exposure, masturbation, and shooting van Gogh-to-Hell in the cornfield.

The blood dripped down onto ripped and dirty pants; demented eyes dying.

Bang, rip, drip.

Boo-boo!

Ah!

Now she's in the house, on the sofa in only her red t-shirt, Little Red Hiding Hood, hiding from the rest of the world, searching through the channels of static on the television. The sun comes in through some cracks in the curtains, a dog barks, that leaf blower won't quit. She can't remember if she's eaten today or not.

Now it's now, and this is how it is:

She's been living in this house for a few months, on the sofa mainly, sometimes sleeping in the bed in nothing but a t-shirt, next to the man who has since shot himself.

They had befriended each other; his wife had died in a one-car accident a year and a half ago. He asked her to move in and he knew he wouldn't be having sex with her. He told her that he just wanted a beautiful woman around, and she needed somewhere to live.

She was moving into his house before she even knew his name (she really needed a place to live); she asked him, as she was bringing in her bag of clothes from her car, "You know something, I don't even know your name. I know you told me, I just forgot."

And he paused, and said, "No, don't worry about it. No name."

"No name."

He nodded.

But they became friends. He called it hell: losing his wife in that crash and now living with Chastity and falling into lust with her and wanting her, but knowing he never would have her. He always knew he couldn't because she always told him no one could.

He had willed the house to her not too long ago, in one of his silent days, when Chastity would hardly see him, even though they'd both be in the house all day, she'd hardly see him.

And when he did, he would listen to her, but was distracted.

Looking back, she thinks he knew that he would end things that way; he might have even had the date planned. She had seen sighs recently; he was either really mellow or really angry, and there really wasn't much in-between. He may scream for an hour and sit there, and shout for one minute and then punch his fist through the kitchen window.

But then he'd be quiet, and sit and stare at the wall in his house, looking out the windows at the empty houses on the street, chain smoking cigarettes. He'd be mellow and nothing would bother him, and at first he'd be quiet but sad, and then quiet and basically neutral in feeling, he'd listen to hours on end to Chastity talking, and then he'd get sad, thinking about his late wife, and then just all angry at the world again, and maybe kick a hole in the wall. But he never kicked or hit Chastity, not until that last night.

He had been nothing but kind to her ever since they met.

She had recently quit her job, or rather had been fired for not showing up. She needed a place to live; they had met in the grocery store where

Thyme worked, while she was shoplifting tampons and carrots ("I'm a virgin, not an angel.").

He didn't have any children with his late wife, and he had no living parents, and his siblings lived across the country, so he had left the house to Chastity in his will.

Now she had a place to live but no money to pay the bills next month; after the canned veggies run out and the power gets cut off, it's time for Plan B, though there was no plan. But for now, she has a place to live, a place to call her own.

She gets up, finds some sneakers, and puts her hair up in a ponytail. She has decided she needs to go back to the hospital to see if Thyme is still there; she doesn't know why, but she feels that she has to go back and see him.

She's walking a few blocks, and a woman about Chastity's age is loading art prints into the back of a station wagon; there are a couple children in booster seats in the back seat. Chastity strikes up a conversation about the print on top, a van Gogh. She tells the woman she was on the way to visit a friend in the hospital; the weather is a little chilly, fall in Richmond, and there was mention of the distance and catching a cold and moments later Chastity is in the front seat of the station wagon being ushered to the hospital.

Chastity smiles and says to her host, the gracious driver, "I shot van Gogh in a corn field, years ago. I shot him dead. I've always been sort of a freak magnet."

The driver looks over at Chastity, slows the car to a stop, and raises an eyebrow and nods towards the door; Chastity gets out.

Chastity turns and heads back home; if she had gone to the hospital she wouldn't have been able to find him, anyway, as he'd been released an hour before. By the time she gets back to the house, it is dark, and Thyme is back at home at his mother's house, crushing pain killers over his oatmeal, stirring them into his soup.

Chapter Sixteen

Two Broken Coffee Mugs and a Busted Nose

Now it's now, and this is how it is:

Thyme has taken some time off from working at the grocery store. It is October; he has harvested his pot plant he had in the yard. Between the pain pills crushed in cereal in the morning and into soup at night, and the buds drying upside-down hanging in the attic, he figures he can get through the burning sensations in his hand until it heals. He'd told work he'd be back in a few weeks, and wasn't even sure if he was going back; he'd been scanning the Classified section in the paper and on line. He realized he didn't have much of a resume, but he looked into a couple ads about working at a one-hour photo booth, and taking portraits at some storefront in the mall that had families come in and dress the kids in matching outfits, and then he figured that would suck.

And he really couldn't do that work right now, with the bandages and the pain; and he still had the pill prescription, with another renewal still available.

Suzanne, Momma Exler, had bought him a new camera as a get-well gift after his camera had smashed on the ground and then vanished from the hospital. It was a nice camera, the best he'd ever had and he was thankful to her and at dinner, after the pain pills in his soup hit his empty stomach, he'd tell Momma Exler about how he'd love to be aboard some helicopter with his camera, somewhere between Pakistan and Afghanistan, taking those pictures that are in the paper and on the internet everyday; but Suzanne would smile, steam rising from her herbal tea, and say, "Ok, but that's just suicide, isn't it?"

And he'd eat his soup, one spoonful of pills at a time, sipping his pain killers.

Suzanne works on staff at the on-line city magazine as a feature writer, and the occasional restaurant review. She was a freelance writer for years, and has published a handful of novels that got decent reviews but never sold too many copies; she'd get a letter from a fan once or twice a year and she never responded to them. She's doesn't write poetry; she can only think of a handful of poems that she even likes or knows the titles of.

She's been working here a little over a year now, at this on-line magazine. She'd written articles for the site here and there in the past and eventually a full-time position was offered to her. At night, on her laptop, she writes chapters of her own novels, and at work she'll send herself plot notes on her email. But she didn't mind this job so much; "All jobs feel like suicide," she says.

She is the only woman working in her office, now that is; the Office Manager is out on an extended maternity leave and the news editor was strangled by her husband in the Fan the day of the Easter Parade last spring.

But she doesn't mind being the only woman; she thinks half the men are gay, and most of the others are married, not that it means anything.

Stan, a man in his early forties, was an ad salesman, and was interested in her and she thought he looked okay. She went out on a date with him and then ended up having sex with him on her kitchen countertop while Thyme was stocking shelves in the grocery. Aside from one instance of fellatio in the stockroom two days later, she's stayed away from him. She didn't get good vibes from him in the time she spent with him, and heard him acting sleazy with a co-worker's wife a couple days later and she decided she didn't want to have anything else to do with him. She really was just interested in him because of his age, she liked to sleep with younger men, and he was almost fifteen years younger than she was. But she had had her fun, so they say, and she had decided to call it off before it went any further. She told him that she wasn't interested in him anymore; he seemed to take it alright. At first he acted as he thought that she was joking, although he knew that she was serious. Then he stared at her for a minute, two, speechless, and made her repeat herself.

It's been a few weeks now since they were on the countertop together, and in that stock room.

And looking back, because of the wine at dinner the time in the kitchen was a bit of a blur, but in the stockroom she was sober, maybe a little preoccupied, and for some reason, his cell phone being in his hand never bothered her. She had her shirt off, and wasn't thinking about the phone at all.

She wants him to stop approaching her in the kitchen; she sees him rub his crotch at his desk, looking at her. He stares at her while he talks on his phone. He stares at her while she talks on her phone.

He begins to park his car as close to hers as he can; even moving it after lunch if Suzanne goes out and parks in a different spot. When Suzanne gets up to go to the bathroom, he watches her; but when she came out, Stan's desk was empty; later that day she watches him try to get a splinter out from under his fingernails and even sends her an email, which she did not reply to, asking if she had any tweezers.

He began to forward nasty joke emails to her, smiling and laughing aloud after he'd sent them and hear the beep for new email on Suzanne's computer. She read them, forwarded to her home email to keep for later, and deleted the email, and went back to whatever she was doing.

She's at her desk at five-fifteen this afternoon; she's thinking about what she's going to cook for dinner, trying to write a few more sentences about a new bar and grill that opened. The service was slow, the c.d. player kept skipping, and the food was no more impressive than she could have done herself.

Then a hand comes up from behind her and gently brushes the hair off of her nape. She feels two fingers slightly caressing the back of her neck, two fingers held together going side to side, moving her hair, making her tingle.

She turns around and there's Stan.

Smiling, Stan's looking down at her, obviously trying to look down her shirt.

"Suzanne, I think you should come by my place later, and come. I have some nice chardonnay."

"I really don't think so, Stan. No."

"How about tomorrow night then?"

"Stan, no. No. It's over, if it ever really started in the first place, it's done now; I don't want to see you anymore, and you're not going to touch me anymore."

He looks hurt. She can tell at first that he has nothing to say, and then he snarls and says "You know, twinkle-tits, you got the wrong answer this time."

He looks down, trying to look into her shirt again, and then spits on her desk, and leaves.

The next morning, she's drinking herbal tea from a coffee mug; she can see Stan has his hand beneath his desk, his arm moving.

Later, they pass in the hall, Suzanne keeps her feet straight and never looks at him, but he says as he approaches her, smiling the whole time, but he doesn't say anything at all to her, he just walks past her, and chuckles softly, and then laughs when he gets further down the hall.

Now it's now, and this is how it is:

This is six o'clock, a couple of days later, and Thyme's gunshot wound is healing, almost healed so far as he can tell.

He's gotten used to the sour taste of Percocet as he crushes one with his molars. No water for a chaser. It gets onto his tongue and throat and his tongue feels heavy. He knows the bandages will be off soon; and he's still a little confused: first, what the hell happened and, two: where was his camera? But he's still got some pills to help the pain and he's supposed to start physical therapy sessions soon, but he thinks he might just skip them. Now he's sitting on the sofa with the remote control in his right hand even though he's not changing the channels.

He likes to make tacos for lunch: he likes to smash up three pain pills with a penny, and then scatter it in the cheese, stick it into the oven and melt it.

He likes to suck on a pain pill as he stares at the news and eats an orange ice cream push up.

It's been a few weeks since Chastity shot him, he watches the news, and fiddles around with his new camera, and is starting to take walks again, not as long as the walks used to be, not yet, not with pain pills in his system.

But it's fall outside and he likes to walk on cool afternoons. Just not too far, in case he gets dizzy from his pills. Or, he laughs to himself, in case he got lost even; lost, so close to home. It's happened before; he laughs and raises his left hand up to eye level. He makes a fist, and it hurts, a lot.

He has hand exercises to do; he's happy his other hand is still strong. He thinks his other hand may have even gotten stronger than it used to be.

He's hungry. He'll go to the kitchen, open a cabinet, pull out a can of tuna, and then open it with the can opener. After he drains out the sick gray liquid, he pulls some pills and a penny from his pocket, puts the coin on the pill, and with his thumb initiates a circle-like movement and crushes the pill, then dutifully gets the entire pill in the tuna still in the can, scoops in a spoon of vegan mayo, and eats it.

He sits now, camera nearby, watching the journalists on television in Iraq, Syria, Israel; Thyme sits on the sofa, holding the remote control in one hand and exercising his shot hand by slowly making fists, then release, fist, release, fist, release.

He eats a pill, crunching it in a handful of trail mix.

He hears the sound of paws scratching on the front door but opens it and sees nothing, but smells dirty fur.

He looks down, dizzy, and sees little drops of water on the concrete steps; drops of drool. He thinks he hears a jingle; he thinks he feels air rush by him.

Now it's now, and this is how it is:

Suzanne is a little late to work today; late to her writing job because she was up late, writing. She's wearing sunglasses, has her hair up, and is carrying a mug with three sips of cold tea in it. She opens the first set of double-glass doors, and then as she's opening the second, to go into the lobby, she drops the coffee mug and tears off her sunglasses.

It is 9:45 a.m. now; people have been coming in the doors for almost two hours and they've all seen what Suzanne's looking at right now: she's looking at color prints of herself, in the supply room, clearly her, topless, with him, Stan, in her mouth. And then there are photos taken from her table in her kitchen, of her on the counter with her legs spread and the nude rear of a man is covering much of her body in the shot, but her head was hanging to the side and as with the other photo, it's clearly her and she's the only recognizable person.

Two men are leaving the building, they pause to look at the photos not sure what they are at first and then they look at her, turn away quickly, and leave through the outside set of doors.

She kicks the mug to the side of the entryway, leaves the pictures where they are, opens the door, and storms down the hallway to the magazine's office. On the door of the office are more shots, these color shots of her, she tears half of these off the front door of the office and opens the doors, going straight to her desk. She stares around the room, and people look at her, and then quickly look away. She stands there, silently, and then gathers a few of her personal items and put them into her purse. No one approaches her; no one calls out to her.

While she's taking cards from her rolodex, she sees Stan at his desk, smiling, not looking at her, both of his hands above his desk this time. She picks up a large coffee mug, one she eats soup from on rainy days, and throws it at him from across the room with more energy than she's used in a decade.

The mug hits his desk and a few clumps of three-day-old soup spurt up onto him, but the mug misses him and keeps going and then shatters into pieces on the floor. Stan sits there, feigning bewilderment.

She stares at him and then says, "Slime," and she picks up her things and turns to leave, walking by the editor's office and offers a simple "I quit" as a farewell.

As she walks through the doors, she takes a cigarette lighter from her purse and sets all of the pictures of her and Stan on fire.

She turns and walks to her car, without looking back.

She already feels better.

Now it is six hours later, nearing the end of the same day:

Thyme, bearded, hair still short, a pill wedged next to his left back molar, a red baseball hat pulled low, left hand still in bandages, walks into the office with a wooden rolling pin in his right hand.

He walks up to the desk that Suzanne had hurled her coffee mug at this morning.

"Stan?"

Stan looks up from his computer screen when he hears his name and simultaneously Thyme swings the rolling pin square into Stan's nose. There is an audible crack, then blood, and Stan falls away from his desk and ends up on his hands and knees, screaming, blood pouring down his chin and onto the floor.

Blood is on the floor and the desk, though not much got on the rolling pin, which Thyme notes pleasantly.

Without a word, Thyme turns and walks out the office, barefoot on the hallway carpet that was dampened by the fire sprinklers that morning. He swallows the pain pill and walks back home.

He smiles as he hears that jingle of the dog tags close behind him.

A squirrel darts in front of him across the sidewalk, and Thyme smiles to himself as he hears that jingle of dog tags race by him and the furry rodent runs up a tree. The squirrel goes halfway up the tree and then turns back, looking down, looking for something and staring at nothing, confusion on its face.

Thyme hears a bark; but sees nothing around him.

He looks around, and seeing no one around, he looks towards the tree, snaps his fingers twice, whistles, and says, "Come on, let's go home."

Wag wag.

The next morning, people passing by the office saw a man, with a bandaged nose, in the hallway scrubbing burn marks off of the door.

His nose would never look the same.

Later still, people going home from work could see Stan carrying a box with photos and a coffee mug, this one not broken, and heading to his car.

He'd been fired.

He's a creep, not a virgin.

Chapter Seventeen

Tennis Balls and Sushi

Now it's now, and this is how it is:

Thyme's outside, with his bandaged left hand and the right hand that just a few days ago put a rolling pin into the nose of a man; he has a red baseball hat on; he has a backpack full of tennis balls.

Since he's been shot, he hasn't spent too much time thinking about why he was shot, or who shot him, or if he was a target, or a misfire. "What's done is done." But he's still upset about the disappearance of his old camera; it's bad enough it had been broken; he could at least keep it in Momma's attic for a memory.

He walks on bare feet to the park; he removes a piece of sidewalk chalk from his backpack, and makes a big X on a tree ("My middle name marks the spot."), the same tree that Chastity was sitting in front of when she shot Thyme.

He's never really played baseball, not since middle school or so: in high school he got interested in photography and films and after high school, he spent his time with Maria, and drugs.

This morning, in between chapters she was working on for her latest novel, Momma Exler opened her closet, and showed Thyme a box full of brand new tennis balls.

"I'd always thought some of your dresses smelled like tennis balls," he said, and she smiled.

"Well, you should always have some fresh tennis balls."

"But, Momma, you don't play tennis."

"You never know when you can use some new balls. I figure they can be your therapy for your hand. Squeeze them. Juggle them. I don't know; I'm not a doctor," and she went off to make a cup of tea and go back to her computer, where she was about seventeen chapters into her newest book.

Now it's now, and this is how it is: Thyme aims the balls at the X he made on the tree, at his middle name, and after he's done throwing them, he picks them up, and then in his left hand, his tender hand, he squeezes one ball at a time as much as he can, but not enough to cause pain. Then with his right hand he does the same, even thought the right hand is not hurt, and then he switches back to his left hand.

He finishes up his exercises for the day and he walks back home, back to where Suzanne, who's back to being a freelance writer, is at home, she's run out in the car and bought some sushi.

"I figured you could use just one hand to eat this, son."

"Yeah, but it's hard to get the wasabi on one-handed."

With a tennis ball in his hand, he remembers how it felt as he swung that rolling pin, the same one that has been in the kitchen since he was a child; he remembers how it felt as it crashed into Stan's nose. Thyme remembers how, at the time, when he was swinging the rolling pin into Stan's then-unbroken nose, Thyme imagined he had a baseball bat in his hands and that Stan's nose was a tennis ball. That was always how he and the neighborhood kids played backyard tennis in Suzanne's backyard, with a tennis ball so it wouldn't break her windows. Thyme recalls having a pleasant warm feeling as he was breaking Stan's nose, but that might have just been the painkillers.

Tonight, after dinner, Suzanne brews a cup of tea and sits at the kitchen table with her laptop and starts to type; she'll be sitting there for a couple of hours, a few even.

Thyme goes out back; the sun is setting but not down, so the sky is the color of a pumpkin near the three lines; on the house, the exterior flood lights are also on, giving the lawn an artificial yellow hue. He walks to the middle of the yard and sits on the picnic table that's rotting: it must be at least twenty years old. He drops a bag of tennis balls at his feet. He's stuffed. He sits with his back to the house and watches the sun set, dipping towards the trees.

He is sucking on an after dinner pill; he crushed it with his teeth and bitter parts get stuck in his molars. His tongue is sour and feels dry. He looks to see if he brought a bottle of water with him; he hasn't.

He has a joint behind his ear, again, and he lights it and smokes it and coughs for a second and the sweet smoke makes the pill taste in his mouth better and the setting sun appears to be setting more slowly, although Thyme knows it isn't.

He doesn't smoke the whole thing before he starts to cough too much and decides to put the joint down on the edge of the picnic table and throw some tennis balls. He's been throwing balls at trees everyday now for a week; he uses his left arm a little, but enough to exercise it some. His aim is good; it's really improved a lot over the past week. He hits almost every tree he aims at, often in the center.

Thyme throws most of them, towards the side yard, and as he gets past the side of the house, he looks over towards the street and sees a car in the road stopped directly in front of his house, and as soon as the driver sees Thyme the car pulls off.

Thyme watches the car drive off, and then collects the tennis balls.

He reaches into his right pocket and pulls out another pill and puts it in his mouth. Then, to help with the bitter taste, he relights the joint, which has gone out, and he smokes the last of it, slowly, slowly burning his fingers, sucking on his pill, and savoring the sweet smoke.

While he smokes, he starts to throw the tennis balls out into the dark parts of the yard, where the flood lights do not light up; the sun is almost down now and the edges of the yard near the trees is dark.

His stomach feels warm and he gets the butterfly feeling again.

His left leg feels it next.

He throws another tennis ball with his right hand, which is feeling heavier, and he is holding the joint in his weak left hand, which is feeling lighter.

On the third throw, he hears that jingle again; it comes from behind him, and it bashes past him and darks out into the darkness of the backyard towards where Thyme threw the ball.

A moment later Thyme hears a faint panting sound in front of him; he bends down and picks up another ball from the ground, smelling fur; he throws another tennis ball and hears the jingle of the collar getting farther away from him, following the ball into the darkness.

When he gets back inside, stoned, Suzanne is still at the table, drinking yet another cup of tea, and she looks up at him, with his distant stare, and says, "You look like you've seen a ghost."

But he blinks his eyes to get his head back into the moment, and then he looks at his mother and says, "No, no, don't worry about it."

And he sits on the sofa, and turns on the television, and is watching the news, and he finds himself falling to sleep mid-news story and waking backup again at the start of a commercial and slipping back into sleep again by the end of the commercial break. He wakes his eyes at the sound of a distant bark outside, but can't decide if he really heard a bark or not and then decides to drift on out again.

As he sleeps on the sofa, he dreams of the conversation he had with Momma not too long ago:
"Do you know what I call things like that?"
"No; what?"
"Painkiller ghosts."

Chapter Eighteen

You Can Go Home Again

Now it's now, and this is how it is:

She's at home; at least that's what she's calling it. This place is hers now; this place where not four months ago she was a stranger, and now she's the owner. The owner of a place with a curse, she's sure. "It isn't really mine," she tells herself, "but I guess it's no one else's either."

Chastity has taken Thyme's stolen and broken camera upstairs and put it in the library.

Thyme's busted camera is on the desk. The lens cap is missing; the lens is shattered.

She's in a new house, her house, her first house. This is like an empty orphanage to her, again: a place to live, a place that somehow just became home.

In the library she looks around the shelves, books lining most of the room. Books. Her books. Her library. The books are arranged alphabetically, more or less. Some places a little less, others a little more. She's glancing through the E's. She reaches and pulls out a thin paperback.

"*Time's Passing*. Suzanne Exler." The book was published twelve years ago, she knows because she opened the book and looked around trying to find a picture of the woman to see, just to see, just in case, if it was the same one she saw in the hospital today. What are the chances, she asks herself, what are the chances?

She takes the book and holds it at her side, and finishes looking through the books, all the way to Z, and then goes to the desk and starts looking through the drawers. Paid phone bills, a five year old porn magazine, blue pens and broken pencils, photographs of people she doesn't know. In the stationary box she found not writing paper but rolling paper and a large bag of marijuana. She smells it and smiles. She takes that from the drawer and puts it on the desk.

She's still in just a t-shirt.

She rolls a joint, then finds some pants, puts them on, and grabs a new-blue bag (one she shoplifted after throwing her old one away in the park) and walks out the door.

On the front stoop, she puts on her shoes. She's got the joint lodged behind her ear and a sweater on. She ties her shoes and walks down the brick steps and then the sidewalk; there are leaves that need to be raked and she doesn't know if she has a rake or not. Or trash bags.

The neighborhood is quiet, no dogs barking, no cars passing. Chastity has noticed this neighborhood is a cemetery. It's dead. She smiles when she realizes that the leaf blower, the one which has been constantly screaming recently, is silent.

She goes out to the end of the sidewalk, looks both directions, and takes off walking to find a new place, a place she's never been before, just to be somewhere new today, just to see something different.

She has the book by Suzanne Exler in her purse.

Now it's now, and this is how it is:

Thyme, tonight being no different than any other, is out walking; the dog collar jingle sounds just a few paces behind him. And being no different tonight than any other night, he's got his camera slung around his neck. It's days like these he likes having a beard, days that are a bit cool, but not cold yet, he doesn't have to wear a jacket, or shoes for that matter, because his beard keeps him warm. That's what he tells himself at least.

Over the past couple of weeks Thyme has kept looking at the photos that he had taken before he was shot. The photo with the person on the roof bothered him.

He's walking on dead leaves. He's walking with his camera, and finally he gets there, to the house. Whose house it is he can't say, but he's there. And he's looking at the front windows, the two dormers upstairs, and it's quiet, and that same car is in the same place that it's been every time and he thinks it must be frozen there somehow, a statue of a car perhaps. And the house is quiet, like all the others around here: dead.

He stands in front of the house, Chastity's house, and he takes a photo.

Then he walks up to the driveway, stepping on leaves the whole way, and he walks up to the sidewalk, and find himself on the brick stairs that Chastity was just tying her shoes on, and he rings the doorbell, he doesn't know why, but he rings the doorbell and knocks on the door, and after one minute, then two he turns around, walking back down the brick steps, back down the sidewalk and driveway. In the street, he looks both ways. There are still no signs of life anywhere. He strokes his beard and walks back down the road the way he came, barefoot on the crushed leaves, four paws following behind him.

Now it's now, and this is how it is:

Stan Thimble and his broken nose sit, sore, swollen, thinking about the job that he lost, chasing codeine pills with a gin and tonic.

He doesn't miss his job. He hated that place anyway, he says to himself, and he's not lying to himself either. He liked the money, liked the fact the office wasn't too far from the university, especially in spring with the co-eds, but he hated the place, didn't read the online downloadable 'magazine' that he worked for, hated his co-workers, he thought most of them were idiots, and all the others he wanted nothing to do with. But he always wanted something from Suzanne. One thing he didn't call her is Momma Exler; he called her things he hadn't said aloud in years.

With her was the first and only time he did it on a kitchen counter, on a first date at that, and he wouldn't forget it. His ex-wife, the bore, would never do it in the kitchen, or on the floor for that matter. With her, his ex-wife, it was always the same. He doesn't miss her, and if he never saw her again, the better.

He didn't mind that he lost his job; he had money in the bank. But his nose: would his nose ever be the same again?

He couldn't believe the insult to injury here. First, Suzanne avoids him, and then she sends some madman to bash his nose in, and with a rolling pin of all things, a wooden rolling pin! He couldn't believe it; he was there at his desk one minute and had a smashed and broken nose the next. Sure he'd put up a few photos of her, but who cares? Men like seeing that sort of thing. All he did was put up a few photos; she didn't have to send some Vinnie-No-Neck in to crush his nose. And a rolling pin? Was the lunatic at home making cookies when Suzanne told him to go and kill Stan? He couldn't figure it out. But he knows she was the cause of this.

She was the cause of his nose being smashed. What did he ever do to hurt her? He didn't hurt her at all.

But her time was going to come, he just knew it.

Chapter Nineteen

It Already Feels Good

Now it's then, and this is how it was:

"I always saw myself as a little girl, just fed and drowsy, being tucked into some basket with a thin blanket and being set into a creek, like a girl baby Moses, with no destination. And I feel that way these days, still."

She's in the living room, she's under her pillows that she's pulled off the couch, and she's Little Red Hiding Hood. She sitting there, talking out into the darkness, to the red light of his cigarette as he's in the dark, before he shot himself on the roof, before he fell onto the driveway, and she's talking to him earnestly; tonight she's not scared about anger, or distracted by his lust.

"I always felt abandoned." She rubs her legs that need to be shaved; she has the other hand in her hair that needs to be cut. "I've always felt like I gamble when I assume I'm going to have someone, anyone, there for me, wherever I am, to fall back onto, to hug for support. Because I don't believe anyone's ever going to be there for me; but, also, I guess that I've never been there for anyone else, either."

He throws her a cigarette and a lighter; she lights a cigarette and does not throw the lighter back to him. He smokes quietly.

She continues, "But the real bitch of it all," and she smiles and then takes a drag off the cigarette, "the real kicker is that I always hated that I was in foster care, but was never actually adopted. I mean," she exhales, "either way I'd feel rootless, but at least if someone had adopted me I'd feel like someone cared. Not just like they wanted some monthly check for keeping kids like me: kids who were sent down the river, with a belly of milk and maybe a kiss goodbye, but probably not."

She stops talking for a minute and stares at the ceiling; he walks over and looks out the window at nothing and then walks back to where he was.

She continues, "I once got curious, and that's a lie, someone I loved once got curious of me," she's lighting a second cigarette, having earlier gotten up from the cushions, in a long t-shirt but no underwear or pants, and opened the front door and flicked the cigarette butt outside, flashing her bare bottom his direction.

"I once got curious, because in my early twenties I met someone I thought was the one. You know: The One. The kind you'd walk in front of a train for? The kind that the rainbow points to? You meet them once in a while. But I was young then. Younger, at least, than now, you know? He said he wouldn't be with me unless we would have kids, and I thought about that. I considered it, a little. But then he told me he'd never have kids unless he knew their background, or lineage, or whatever." She smiles, laughs a little, "Like stupid fluffy poodles in a dog show I guess. I don't know; I don't care anymore."

Ash falls onto the floor. She's still rubbing her legs. He's quiet; smoke hovering around his head.

"So I got on-line a little, but this was what, a decade ago and the internet wasn't quite like it is now, but I got a phone number and mailing address, back in the nineties sometimes that's what a good internet site provided, and I started looking into it. Turned out to start a search for some information into natural parents, and not even like their names or whatever, just to find out if they were Croatian or Cuban or Cherokee or I don't know what else, well it cost a lot of money and that's something I don't have now and definitely didn't have then. But I wrote a bad check and I sent it in and it was cashed and the bank paid it and I got all sorts of fees and they shut down my checking account soon afterwards, and the agency still couldn't give me any information. They blamed it all on bad paperwork prior to computers, back when the staff wasn't trained back in the seventies; to them it was a long time in terms of records, documents; a lot were lost and mine were apparently among those."

She stops for a minute and stares out the windows at the dark houses on the street.

"Yeah, sometimes I'd like to know a little bit about them, the people who are my parents. And that sounds funny to me, parents, because I don't have parents, but I must have parents. How funny. Sometimes I'd like to know a little bit about them, but most of the time, no, I don't think about it.

"You don't really think about something like that if you never had it. It's not like I lost my parents; I don't have any. I never had any. In fact, I have no kin. None at all.

"I don't know what hospital I was born in, and I'm not too certain about the town, either. I can't remember if one of my foster parents told me things, or if over time I just told myself so much stuff it just became real in my head.

"But then, why would I want to find out anything about them, these so-called parents of mine, maybe to find out if there's any chance of heart disease, maybe cancer, but that's it really."

She lights her last cigarette of the day, and stops rubbing her legs.

"But do you know what I'd say if one, or both of them, came up to me and introduced themselves? Do you know what I'd say?"

They both smoke; he's still quiet in the dark, still the red end of the cigarette and the smoke are the only sign of him. He silently shakes his head, no.

"I'd lie. I'd look at them and lie and say, 'I never needed you,' and then I'd turn my back, and walk away forever. Like they did to me. That's what I'd do and that's what I'd say and I bet it would feel good. Real good.

"In fact, it already feels good." She's smiling now, exhaling smoke from her nose, a gleam in her from her cigarette and her thoughts. "It already feels good."

She goes on: "And then, and this I never thought about until I was a teenager, at the age when most girls are going on dates and having boys feel them, this is what happened, I began to notice that if I was attracted to a guy, he had similar characteristics as myself. Physically, not personality. But the same eye and skin color, same textured hair, same fingers and nose. And then I woke up one day thinking that these guys that I was attracted to could very well be related to me somehow, we were in the same state, same part of the state, I thought it was a chance that I didn't want to take. I didn't want to accidentally sleep with my brother. And that's where I'm forever trapped, in a way. I think when most men and women meet they ask themselves if they find the other person attractive, sexually, and then most likely make sure that this person isn't say, their cousin. Or brother. I can never do that."

And on: "In those dreams, when my parents show up, they're always different:

"Sometimes, they would be a happy couple, all smiles, looking just like me, and they'd have four or five of their kids with them, and here's the kicker, half the kids will be older than me, and the other half younger . . . and I look at them and think 'Why them? Why not me?' And all the others, my siblings, my lost brothers and sisters, will look at me and laugh at me and that's when I'll lie and say 'I never wonder about you' and close the door.

"Other times, it's just two people, a woman, a man, and they're dressed well and tall and all but faceless, not headless, but faceless. I open the door, and where there should be a mouth, nose, eyes, it's as if they've pulled their necks up to cover their face's features. And they try to hug me. And I tell them 'I don't want you', and I close the door and they don't knock, they turn and leave. I lie to them; I lie to them about missing them, about wanting them.

"And then sometimes, it is just a man, holding a photo of a woman that I look a lot like; he's knocking on the door, there are tears in his eyes, he sees me and cries out 'It's just like your mother, alive again, bless her soul, you're her, alive again.' And he stops looking at me and just looks down at the photo and cries and cries and then refuses to look at me and turns and leaves, not saying anything else, and for him abandoning me, again, I look at him descending the sidewalk and because he didn't tell me anything new, or at all even, I watch him leave and whisper 'I don't care about you', and then I start to feel better, it already feels good just talking about it, maybe I'll have another dream about them.

"Three days ago, I had a dream that I was at the beach, and it was chilly, too cold for many people to be on the beach, only some walkers, joggers, maybe a cop on an ATV once in a while. I was in a sweatshirt, I can't remember what color, but I want to think green, and I was in a pair of jeans, I remember feeling that I'm chilly, the wind is coming from out over the ocean, and it's just freezing, it burns my cheeks, especially when it whips up the sand and it all hits me; in my dream I even have the grit from sand in my teeth, it crunches in my mouth; I'm standing there, facing towards the wind, watching the waves, the white foam, the birds holding still mid-air in the tremendous Nor Easter gusts. And then I notice something in waves, floating around, getting pushed in and then back out, and that's when I think that it's shaped like a body. But it must be a child or a woman, because it's not too big, and it appears clothed. I get up; I've got cold sand in my nose, in my hair, in my ears. I can feel the grit. I walk down to the beach, and I flip off my shoes, and hold my pants up a little, but still get wet, and I walk a little into those cold, dark waves and then, yes, it is a body and not a child, but a woman. And I'll be ready to scream when I notice that she's smiling, and her eyes are open, and she looks just like me, just older, and bloated from drowning. And I know it's her. It's my mother. She doesn't move, or say anything, she's dead. Real dead. My lost mother found, and still dead to me, and I'll lie again and say 'I won't miss you' and with my left foot kick the fish-eaten bloated skin back into the waves and I run and run and go get somewhere safe and it feels good. It felt like I buried her myself, however odd and sick that sounds. But I already feel warmer. Stronger. Better.

"It already feels good."

"And something else that's hard for people to get over," she's still talking to the man, now very dead like the mother in the water in her dreams, he's still smoking, he's not worried about cancer, she's still talking, she's not thinking about suicide, "is when I'm sitting in a bar, and I know I'm good looking, but let's be straight here, I know that guys just want to put their dicks in me, and not just me, in any woman." There's a smile from across the room. "But I'll go to a bar, I go alone a lot, I'll buy my first drink and then some guy, older, will buy my next one and he'll say something like 'I'm a lawyer, what are you?' and what can I say back? I'm not some scholar, not a model, not a mother, not a wife, not a Christian, not a Jew, not an artist, not a graduate; I don't even have a job. So I'll tell them what I am. I'll tell them 'I'm an orphan' and they squirm. 'I'm a rootless, drifting orphan.'

"They squirm in their seats, especially the men who are, say fifteen to twenty-three years older than me, you can see it in their eyes, behind the glaze from the beer and the smoky bar air, you can see them looking at me and making sure I don't look familiar, they're never really sure what happened to that girl they banged three times in one week a long time ago who just disappeared. They squirm like a bug.

"And then I make them really squirm, I tell them I'm a virgin. They're looking at me, unemployed, a thirty-something virgin, but dressed showing cleavage to pay my way home with, if I need to, and they drink their beer, quickly, and leave. They usually end up being cheap tippers anyway, I always feel sorry for the bartenders."

She just looks at the ceiling for a bit, smiling at memories.

She goes on, "So if these people, two of them, walked into this room, over to this sofa, and tried to talk to me, tried to explain themselves to me this is what I'd have to do: I'd have to take a deep breath and say 'You're never in my dreams' to them. That's what I'd say, I'd lie, and it would feel good, so good.

"It already feels good and I haven't even done it yet."

She'd lie.

And it already feels good, so good.

Chapter Twenty

It Still Feels Good

She goes on: "My very first memory is having three pennies in the right pocket of my favorite corduroy pants; I rubbed those three copper coins together until they got worn down. It's funny: I don't remember if I found those or if someone gave them to me."

She stops and sneezes, rubs her nose, blinks her eyes, and goes on: "Maybe I stole them. Maybe I stole those three pennies. I mean, I'm a virgin, not an angel. But I had those three pennies in my pocket, and I was rubbing them together, hard, with my right hand. It's funny, memory; because sometimes you remember something one way but you know it couldn't have been so. See, I was so young that no way would I have been able to maneuver three coins around themselves, especially in little pockets with one hand. My foster father from the time had the other hand, my left one. I bet I was just holding them close, in my fist. He was holding my other hand, and that was okay with me, but as I remember they were all okay with me, just okay. But also, as I know, memories aren't always right."

She stops for no reason. Stares out the window towards the dark houses across the street, notices that no cars are passing by, no kids are outside playing, no leaf blowers are blowing, and no long-absent parents are looking for her.

"So, my first thought, my first memory I should say, is standing there, with the coins in my right hand and a man's hand holding my left hand, and it's chilly, a little later in the year than it is now, and we're looking down at a grave. The image is hazy, sure, a bit like junior year of high school, it's hazy but it's still there. I know I was looking down at the grave of a child, you could just tell. Children's headstones just have a different feel than the others. A glow. And it's not just the lambs carved into the white marble, or the naked smiling angels, there's just a difference to the feel. So I know that's what I was seeing, and I know who the child was: it was his. It was his daughter. And I knew that the reason that he had me as a foster child was because he wanted a child of his own, but he didn't want me, or any other foster kid for that matter. He wanted a child of his own, and no other child would bring her back.

"That first thing, the graveyard, the coins, my left hand being held by his right hand, the real flowers dying on the graves around us, the leaves that needed to be raked. And me, there, as a substitute. I felt for the first time what I would later know to be inadequacy. And some might say that feeling stuck around for a while, a very long while even. And I might be one of those that said it."

No Name smiles; so does Chastity. They make brief eye contact.

She continues, "So, there I was, rubbing those pennies together, all of a sudden feeling like, I don't know, like a burden. And I remember pulling those three pennies out of my pocket, and throwing one as hard as I could away from me one direction, and then another the other way, and then eating the last penny. I just put it in my mouth, and swallowed it and I remember that it did have a taste. A metallic, dirty taste. A warm metallic taste. And I stuck it in my mouth and swallowed right after I tossed the other coins in opposite directions and then I gagged but I got the coin down, down into my stomach.

"Later, a couple years I guess but I can't be sure, and neither can anyone I know, but later I drew a picture, a stick figure picture, and it was of me with my arms spread out and two pennies floating away from my somewhat open palms and my tongue was stuck out and I had a penny on my tongue, and there were lumps which were supposed to be headstones, but there was no father in the picture. No foster parent. I was there, alone, among the stones, the graves, and about to choke in the picture.

"But I kept that drawing for years, and I remember, later on, in a different home, a different city, I took a red crayon, newly sharpened, and I drew the man back into the picture. I drew him back in, he was in red, and I was in brown, but I drew him in and then with the same crayon I drew a red smile onto my brown face. And I remember that then I felt happy. I remember that all of a sudden it felt so good. It felt good, so good.

"And it still feels good. I don't need them. I don't need them, not now."

She's silent for a long time, so is the man across the room from her. He's there leaning against the wall, feeling excited looking at the girl across the room from him, the one who's a virgin, not an angel, the one who used the red crayon.

He says something to her, one of the last things he'll say to her, and he says, "I want you to remember, Hiding Girl, I want you to know what it's like for me: I can't feel like me in this world. Not anymore. You just seem so free to me. I just can't feel like me anymore."

Brief eye contact, she nods, and they look away from each other.

This is the last time that we will see into her past, now that she's decided she doesn't need to have one, and that feels good, it feels so good.

That was then, and this is the end of then:

Thyme is outside, walking down the street in his bare feet, his camera, as always, with him. The silence in this part of the neighborhood calms him, he's thinking about his Momma, he's thinking about Maria, he's thinking about the dog they used to have, the one that died but is still three paces behind him, and then he's thinking about how many exposures he has in his camera and about how he loves this time of year so much.

This is the last time we'll see into Thyme's past.

There is no longer any past for Thyme.

There is no longer any past for Chastity.

And it feels good to them.

It already feels good.

Part Three

Photography, Unemployment, & Otherwise Popping Pain Pills

Chapter Twenty-one

Noses Are For Breaking

Now it's now, a few weeks later, and this is how it is:

Stan Thimble is done with his codeine prescription for his broken nose. He chewed his last two with a handful of raisins and peanuts an hour ago.

It seemed to Stan that his nose had been broken more than not over the past forty-some years.

Most of the broken noses were from bar fights, or fights at drinking parties. Some were due to a few youthful games of touch football, field hockey, or rugby. And there were, of course, the car crashes. There were always car crashes. But, more or less, he's come out unscathed, except for the habitually smashed nose.

His left nostril always bleeds longer than the right one, and it always starts bleeding first.

The first car crash was when Stan was sober, more or less, and a drunk driver took a turn and went head first into his car. Stan walked away; the other driver went through the windshield. Then the second one was when Stan was drunk, more or less, and a fifteen year old kid, with no license and in his parent's car, veered the same way on the same curve in the same place three years later and once again, Stan's left nostril bled a lot longer than the right one and the kid never walked again.

Bent, busted.

Broken.

And the left side always bleeds longer.

He wanted to hit Suzanne Exler, but he always wanted her, again.

'Imagine,' he reasoned to himself, 'doing someone who had her son crush your nose.'

It's her fault. In his head it is. It's Suzanne Exler's fault that his nose is broken and his pain pills are gone and his Cobra plan is expensive and he hates looking for a job. And he got fired because of her. What he'd give to do her again, on that kitchen counter, and this time, to slap her afterwards; to slap her in the face, hard.

What was the big deal?: they were just pictures.

He turns the volume on the television off, then on, then back off, keeping the image on the screen. He gets up from his chair, steps on the newspaper, and walks outside.

He thinks he'd rather have a bandaged nose now than in summer, with the women jogging by in virtually nothing. He'd rather have a busted nose now when scarves are almost out of the closet and people are more worried about the leaves on the ground than their neighbor with the messed up nose who isn't going to work anymore.

And he thinks about Suzanne Exler, and lies aloud, "I don't dream about you."

Then he thinks, "It already feels good."

Chapter Twenty-two

Free Money and Painkiller Soup

Now it's now, a couple of days later, and this is how it is:

Thyme's gotten a new prescription. He kept on complaining to the doctors about the burning pains longer than he needed to. When asked on a pain scale from 1 to 10 he'd always look at the doctor and say, "This is embarrassing because I've been shot before . . . but it's an seven, maybe a six," when really it was a four, maybe a three.

And it's that time of year. He's harvested his plant in the back. He cut it down, trimmed off the leaves, and hung it upside down in the attic for a week, and then stuck it in a shoebox after that and now would cut off crystal-filled red-haired green puffs. Between the painkillers and the weed, Thyme experienced a month of the in-and-outs. He found days where he'd wake up, crush Percocet onto a grapefruit, eat it, and then pack his glass pipe with herb, and would be in-and-out of sleep all day; when he wasn't out, he was still in a haze. He found it was a battle to stay up until noon.

He watches the nature channels for hours now; he can no longer take the news.

And now it's time for a Fig Newton, cut open and packed with two and a half Percocets; he's daydreaming in the day, tossing in his bed at night. When he's alone, he speaks aloud when he means to be talking in his head; at night, eating painkiller soup, he thinks he's said something aloud to his mother, but instead he's asked himself silently, in his head.

He finds himself talking to the ghost of a dog that's he's convinced is there; he's not sure it's there all the time, but sometimes he's sure.

Is it time for another?

Yet?

Conversely, Chastity has been keeping her bag of pot mostly untouched, mostly. That joint she had behind her ear the other day she gave away, over on Cary Street, to one of the bearded vets asking for change.

Thyme's fallen asleep, bearded and burnt, and just before noon; Chastity is out for a walk. She has nothing else to do, nowhere to go.

She has her blue bag with her, her new blue one; she's still got the book by Suzanne in her bag. Chastity has never been a big reader, but she's working her way through it. Mostly she reads magazines; she loves the paper.

She walks down to the park, the one where she shot Thyme. It's not too sunny but she has sunglasses on. She walks past the grounds keepers, the two of them are sitting on a golf cart, drinking sodas. They both look at her twice, they can't quite place her but know they've seen her.

She walks past the tree where she was sitting when Thyme was shot. There's a faint chalk X on it. She keeps going into some small woods. It's on a hill and she can hear a train nearby.

She sees a large tree with some branches about waist high and heads that direction. She climbs up to a limb, sits, and pulls the book out, and begins to read.

After a while a squirrel gets her attention, dropping an acorn or something from above, and she looks down at the ground, where it fell, and sees brown leather. It's a wallet. She picks it up. She opens it and pulls out sixty dollars in twenties, pulls out a MasterCard, pockets those, and keeps the wallet in her hand. She puts the book into her bag, on top, spine sticking out.

She's passing by the grounds keepers in their cart, they're done with their sodas and sitting there, not doing anything at all.

"I found this, over there, in the woods." She hands them the wallet. They still don't quite recognize her with the sunglasses on. She turns and walks down the path, through the stone columns, over the parking lot, and starts to walk home.

She's a virgin, not an angel.

Now it's now, and this is how it is:

Stan Thimble's left nostril has finally stopped bleeding.

It started bleeding this morning in the kitchen, right after he had taken off the bandages for the first time since the rolling pin incident. He had left the bathroom after taking off the bandages, more painful that he had expected, and was not paying attention and walked nose-first into a kitchen cabinet he had left open.

The left nostril bled onto the floor and dripped back down the hall as he ran and held the same bandages he had just taken off up to his bloody nose. But now, it's finally stopped bleeding. He keeps the nose bandaged. He'll try to take them off again tomorrow.

But now, he needs some beer, cheese, a sausage pizza, crackers, canned spinach, and aspirin, lots of aspirin.

He'd also have to find some screws to hang the cabinet door back up; after he walked back into the kitchen he tore the door off its hinges. But first, time to get some beer.

Now it's now, the next day, and this is how it is:

Thyme's trying to stay awake until 11 a.m.

He doesn't think he'll make it.

Chastity thinks about trying to use the credit card to get some gas in her car. But she decides against it. She's afraid of getting caught. She's not sure if there's any investigation into Thyme being shot, but she doesn't want to attract attention to herself. Again.

She chickens out of using the credit card, but drives to the store with what gas she has left to get food.

Inside the store, she sees a man picking up canned veggies, and he's got a bandage over his nose. Part of it, his left nostril side, is red; the right side is coming loose.

She walks over, she's to his right, just her purse between then; she's looking at all of the cans. So many types. All the same. She's reaching to pick one at random and hears, "You reading that?"

"What?" She looks at the man with the bandaged nose, looks at the can in her hand, and then down to her purse, "Oh, yeah, I am, a little."

"I read it."

He just stares at her bag, at the spine of *Time's Passing* sticking up. She smiles, he's not looking at her, just the book, she asks, "What did you think of it?"

He looks up; looks her in the eye: "I was really let down. Not my style." He smiled and looked down again. "But she's got potential; I'm excited about trying her again."

He winks at her, grabs one more can, turns, and walks off.

She walks down the bread aisle, grabs a loaf, then some bagels. Next she gets some cheese. She gets there right after the same man, the bandaged one, had grabbed some sharp cheddar and disappeared into the beer section.

She finds some provolone, walks away, through the empty aisles, and up to the register, where Erin is standing, writing on a clipboard. Chastity gives her some of the cash she'd taken out of the wallet, gets her change, takes her bags and walks out of the door.

A few minutes later, the bandaged man walks up to the register, takes his items out, beer, cheese, canned items, pizza, crackers, and two bottles of aspirin.

He looks Erin in the eye, smiles as big as he can without making his nose bleed more, and says, "Hi, I'm Stan."

Chapter Twenty-three

Passing Thyme and a New Bottle of Pills

Stan meets Erin for dinner and drinks the next day at 7:15.

They meet on the corner of Main and Meadow (near where Chastity was when she shot that man) and they walk down the street and go to a new bar.

Stan's taken off his bandage, but he has some extra in his pocket, just in case the left nostril starts to bleed again. It always does. Erin can't decide if she would have preferred him to keep it on or take it off. With it on, he looked like he just had plastic surgery maybe; with it off, it looked like he had been hit in the nose with something hard, like a baseball bat.

Walking down the street, she asked him a couple things. She asked him what his last name was, what happened to his nose. He answered, "Thimble. I know, it's a wimpy name, ha ha. Just got hurt in an accident, that's all. I should have been wearing my seatbelt." He tried not to smile too much because it still hurt to smile.

Appetizer is calamari. A couple light draft beers. Then salads, they laugh and exchange glances when they order the same salads and same dressing. Then a couple brown ales. "So, you haven't told me what you do, Stan."

"I'm kind of between things now. Enjoying a little freedom."

He finishes off his drink. He orders them both a glass of red wine, to go with their dinners. Steaks arrive. Earlier, Stan told Erin he respects a woman who eats a steak on a first date.

"I guess you don't have to ask what I do."

"No, I guess I know already."

"It wasn't supposed to be this long; I've been there for years, somehow."

He tries the wine.

She continues, "It was only supposed to be for a little while, to pay off some bills." She takes a sip of her wine; they both nod in unison about the wine. "I still haven't paid off some of those bills." And with that they both take a second sip. "What did you do? When you had a job."

"Sales."

"For who?"

"Oh, some website, it wasn't my scene there; so I quit."

The steaks arrive.

She raises her wine glass is the air, "Well, cheers, Stan. Cheers: Here's to breaking free."

He raises his red wine to hers; they clink, "Cheers," he says and takes two sips of his wine.

The steak is good. Very good. It's the best steak he can remember having in a while. And he's sitting across from a woman who's pretty and almost ten years younger than he is. Stan thought to himself, it's a good day. His nose was feeling better, more of a constant pressure than the radiating pain that went out every time his heart beat. But he was careful not to sneeze, which would start the bleeding again; he told the waiter twice not to put any pepper on the steaks or the salads.

She ate about three-quarters of her steak; he, all. She ate her roll that came on the plate; he didn't touch his.

She's drinking the rest of her wine; he's ordering two gin and tonics for them. She's saying, "You know I really would love to just quit my job, do something else, or really not do anything at all for a while, travel, maybe even just sit on the sofa for a month." She turns her eyes to the bar, looks down at her empty wine glass, back to the bar, and to Stan. "Oh, no, not here."

"What?" Stan turns his head towards the bar.

"No, no. Don't stare. I just know one of those guys over there. I try to stay away from him."

Thyme's waking up from a nap that started during the six o'clock news. It's past 8 p.m. It's dark outside. There's no traffic on the street, no sounds in the kitchen, there are no sounds in the house at all since the television is on mute. He rubs his eyes, looks around, his beard itches. It takes him a moment to figure out where he is, what time it is, morning or night? He never bothers with what day it is; it means nothing to him right now.

He listens in the house, hears nothing. Suzanne must be out.

He hasn't walked today; he spent the whole day in a painkiller haze, just like the other day, and yesterday. And tomorrow. He stands up, and sits back down. In a minute he'll try again.

He stands up a little slower after a moment of watching the news with the sound off. A little slower this time, and no head rush now. He picks up a sweatshirt from the floor next to the sofa, pulls it over his head, and walks to the bathroom.

When he comes back, he finds his keys, puts them in his left pocket of his worn khakis, the same pair he wore yesterday, and picks up the camera, slings it over his shoulder, and walks out the front door, barefoot, the cement still warm from the sunlight even though the air is cool.

He whistles, quietly.

He stops and listens for a minute for that familiar jingle of dog tags, and then when he doesn't hear the sound for a minute he starts walking, slowly. And then, less than twenty paces away, he hears it, the sound, catching up with him.

Suzanne pulls into the driveway just as Thyme turns the corner and walks off, into the night. She walks in, carrying a pair of new shoes, and a bag from a bookstore. She's bought two travel books, one for Costa Rica and one for a Pacific island she's never heard of.

Chastity's at her house now. She eats canned vegetables and a bagel for dinner and then smokes a joint and watches a French movie with no subtitles.

She doesn't know French.

It's 9 p.m.

Back at the bar, Stan hasn't looked back in the direction that Erin was looking, and she's tried her best not to look over there either. They talk awhile and Stan forgets about the guy at the bar; Erin hasn't. Stan needs to use the bathroom, so he excuses himself, and wanders to the back of the room and down a hall.

He has to wait in the hallway, it's a one-man room, and the door is locked. A couple minutes later the door open and a woman walks out, smiles at Stan, and walks off. Stan checks the door again to make sure it's the men's room; it is. He closes the door behind him.

A few minutes later, walking down the hall and drying his hands on his pants, he sees someone leaning over his table, talking very close to Erin's ear. She's shaking her head 'No' but not saying anything.

Stan taps the guy on his shoulder. The guy turns, looks at Stan's nose.

Stan goes on, "Hello," he says to the man, then eye contact to Erin and "Is everything alright?"

Erin shakes her head no.

Stan says, "Leave her alone." He smiles, and pats the man's shoulder, "Thanks."

The man walks off towards his seat at the bar, but first he turned back and stared at Erin for ten seconds.

Stan had been about an inch taller; but for a second there he was scared that he was going to get punched in the nose. He had a phantom taste of painkillers on his tongue.

About ten minutes later, Stan notices the man walk out the front door, with a half full beer bottle in his hand, turn left, and walk down the street past the front windows of the bar and out of sight.

They order one more drink each, spiked coffees, and a piece of pie too; she orders a key lime and he a pecan slice. The coffee comes and it's not too weak; the pie is great. Stan pays, in cash, and leaves a nice tip to impress Erin. She goes to the restroom while Stan goes outside front of the bar and waits.

He's walking around the sidewalk out front, checking his voice mails, hoping for a message about a job. He's about three doors down with the cell phone to his right ear, when a shadow jumps out from the alley next him, with a broken beer bottle, and slashes it across Stan's left ear, then trips him, and Stan falls onto the sidewalk.

Stan recognized him of course. It was the guy from the bar; he hadn't even put on a hat or sunglasses. Stan's bleeding; his ear is burning in pain, throbbing, hot. The guy was out of sight, back down the alley.

Stan figured it was best that Erin was inside, maybe the drunk jerk just meant to get Stan, or maybe he was thinking that Erin was there with him too. He hears steps behind him, heels, slower and then faster; Erin sees Stan on the sidewalk.

"Stan?" She runs down the uneven sidewalk as fast as she can in her heels. "What happened?"

She helps him up; he's holding his hand up to his ear and hasn't said anything yet, and she says, "Come on, get in my car."

They get in her car and pull away from the curve, with one tail light out.

Thyme's been out on a walk more than an hour. He's wide awake, the most awake he's been in days. He realizes he didn't smoke much pot today; not as much as normal. His feet, for the first time in a long time, are getting cold. He's off the sidewalk, walking down the deserted street, occasionally getting poked by broken pine cones underneath his calloused feet.

With his new camera, he can more or less pick it up and hold the weight with his right hand, and with his right index finger he hits the auto focus. He snaps off pictures of cars as they go past him.

He's at a crosswalk. He's crossing over from one side to another, it's a four way stop. He pauses and starts walking, assuming that the red car coming quickly in his direction will stop, or at least pause, at the stop sign.

It doesn't.

It seems to speed up. Thyme has to hurry across the street to avoid getting hit by the speeding car. He turns his head just in time to see the driver look left and then right, looking for other cars but never seeing Thyme. It's dark, but it looks like Erin driving. He tries to see better but the car is gone.

He lifts his camera in his right hand, forgets to hit auto focus, and captures a frame of the red car with a broken tail light.

He looks down to his left, where his old dog would be heeling next to him, and says, quietly, under his breath, "Did they almost hit you, boy?"

Now it's now, two hours later, and this is how it is:

Stan's leaving the hospital. He's got a new bottle of pills, ten stitches, and a new bandage over his left ear. Ten stitches and a new bottle of pills; that kind of evens out in the end, he thought.

Erin waited for him the whole time; laughed with him as he filled out the forms, sat in the waiting room, watching cable news when he was behind closed doors.

She walks him out to the car, closes the door after him, walks around and gets in the driver seat, looks over and sees his bandaged ear, and smiles, saying, "You look like Vincent van Gogh."

He smiles; he's not much of an art fan.

The red car leaves the parking lot, driving towards Stan's house; he's going to leave his car near the bar tonight and get it tomorrow, if it hasn't been towed. He directs her to his house, left here, next right, that second one there, park here.

She walks him to the door. He has to go back to the car as he'd left his new pills in it; the burning pain in his ear as he walked to the front door reminded him of them. He comes back and Erin says, "Aren't you going to ask me in for a night cap or something?"

"I'm not sure if I have any night caps here. Not even one beer."

"I don't really care about the night cap . . . just invite me in, van Gogh, genius."

He does; she goes in. He puts his keys, wallet, and pill bottle down; she takes off her shoes and walks to the kitchen. She's taking off her shirt on the way in.

Stan follows her into the kitchen. The only thing in his pockets is his cell phone. He takes it out and he enters the kitchen, puts it on the table on top of some magazines, then takes off his shirt.

Stan takes Erin right there on the kitchen counter top, the same one that his wife would never do it on, and as he did Erin on that counter, he thought about being in Suzanne Exler's kitchen, about being with Suzanne. He thought about that the whole time.

After they're done, while Erin's in the bathroom, Stan gets a glass of water and swallows down two of the new pills; he's happy his nose didn't start bleeding right there in the kitchen, between thrusts. But there's no blood on his face, and there's a woman walking around the house with nothing but a bra on, and the pills will kick in soon to help with the fire in his ear, and he sat and thought about Erin, and Suzanne.

And he felt good.

Real good.

Chapter Twenty-four

Good Morning, van Gogh, Sweetie Freaky

Now it's now, the next morning, and this is how it is:

Stan doesn't feel as good right now as he did when he went to bed: with a painkiller (or two) in his stomach. He doesn't feel quite as good as he did last night, but that can be changed in a few minutes.

He wakes up first; Erin's asleep in his bed.

The first thing he does is go to the kitchen, next to the sink, he opens the spice cabinet, with the sage, cumin, paprika, pepper, vitamins, and pill containers and he grabs the new one, for his sliced ear, and he takes off the top. He takes out a pill, just one, and he swallows it, then turns on the facet in the sink and leans down and swallows that pill with the first tap water of the day.

He grabs a grapefruit and a cutting board (a bamboo one) and slices the grapefruit in two, cuts out each section individually, and then puts the knife down. He lays down two paper towels, takes out two more pills, and sandwiches the pills between the paper towels. He opens one drawer, the one with the silver wear, and then he closes it and opens the one next to it, the ones with the knives and wine openers. He takes out a wooden mallet, a crab hammer. He hates this mallet. The end is always coming off, getting loose. He hates it because he got it on his honeymoon with his ex-wife. And then he hits the pills two, three, four times; he hits them straight down, and lifts the mallet up, so as to not tear off parts of the paper towels into the pills. He puts the mallet down. He takes off the top paper towel, makes sure no crumbs of pills are there, and balls it up and throws it towards the trashcan and misses. He lifts up the other paper towel, into a u-shape, and he holds it above the grapefruit slices and taps the small chunks of Percocet pills down. Stan throws the paper towel in the trash. He opens a cabinet to the right and pulls out a sugar bag, he pours some from the bag straight down onto the grapefruit. He puts the sugar away, now grabs a spoon, takes one bite and puts the spoon down to rest on the fruit.

He pulls the coffeemaker forward onto the counter more and plugs it in. He keeps the coffee in the fridge, so he opens it and grabs it from next to the orange juice and old milk. He turns on the tap, gets a cup, and fills it with water. He pours the water in the coffee maker, takes a bite of grapefruit, and then fills the cup with water again.

He opens another cabinet and gets a coffee filter, puts it in the coffee maker, then spoons some ground coffee beans into the filter. He takes another bite of grapefruit. He closes the top of the coffee maker; he twist ties the coffee shut and puts it back into the fridge. He turns on the coffee maker, and takes another bite of the grapefruit.

He turns and walks across the room and grabs his cell phone from where it was watching Erin and him on the counter across the room; he takes the phone and plugs it into its charger next to the coffee maker. He takes another bite of the grapefruit.

He hears the floor squeak behind him.

"Good morning, van Gogh, Sweetie." Erin smiles, and winks at Stan, who almost forgets about the bandage on his ear, until his left nostril starts to bleed again.

Thyme wakes up and has to look around and determine where he is and then he can determine what happened last night.

He's in the den on the sofa and waking up to one of the home shopping channels, its six-thirty-seven in the morning. He closes his eyes but can't go back to sleep. At six forty-five, he gets up. He walks into the kitchen and opens the fridge, takes out a bottled water, a nice cold water, open its, puts the top on the counter, and drinks about one-third of it.

Again, it's time. He goes to the closet, finds his sweatshirt, and then pulls a glass pipe and a baggie from the pocket. He's got a lighter in the khaki pants he's wearing from last night. He opens the baggie. Nice, fresh green buds, with crystals he can see, and red hairs, and when he touches it and smells his fingers the smell lingers. He knows he shouldn't be keeping it in a bag, in his pocket, it's too good; but he's got some more.

He puts the sweatshirt on, the one that he took his stash from, and he opens the back door, heads out on the deck in the back, and closes the door behind him. He can see his breath. It's a little dark still, or maybe it's just a little light. He has the glass pipe in his right hand, his good hand. He puts it down. He takes the lighter out of his right pocket. Then he picks up the pipe with his left hand, not too firm, because he needs his right hand for the lighter.

He thinks that sometimes the big bowls never last too long, and he goes inside, puts the pipe back into the pocket of the sweatshirt, and he takes off the sweatshirt and drops it onto the floor in the closest.

He walks over to the cabinet next to the sink, open it, and grabs a coffee mug. He turns the sink on and watches it for a minute, a minute and a half until some steam starts to rise off the bottom of the sink and then he fills the coffee mug with the hot tap water, not quite to the top.

He gets a tea bag from the other cabinet, sticks it in the mug of water, and opens the microwave. He programs in one minute and twenty seven seconds and presses Start with his right hand.

He stares into the microwave for the whole time, almost a minute and a half and he watches the mug turn in a circle on the carousel in the microwave.

It beeps and startles him.

He continues to stare into the microwave for a second, two, five. Then he reaches up, with his right hand, the good one, and opens the door, takes the mug out, it burns his fingers a little, and he puts it down quickly on the glass range below.

He opens another cabinet and takes out a salad bowl. He opens the same cabinet that had the sugar in it and he takes out a box of grits. Instant grits, one minute in the microwave. He opens the fridge, searches for some butter and milk. He finds vegan butter and organic milk. He takes some sea salt, and mixes it, and puts the bowl in the microwave. Two and a half minutes. He presses the Start button and then he grabs his sweatshirt from the closet floor, puts it on, opens the door and goes out and smokes another pipe full.

When he comes in, the beeper is going off.

He opens the microwave and takes out the grits, puts them on the counter, picks up a spoon, and stirs them. He adds a little more salt.

He picks up a pencil that has dropped on the floor. He holds it in his right hand, his good hand. He walks to the drawer to the left of the silver wear, opens it, and pulls out a white legal pad of paper.

He blows on his tea; he takes the tea bag out of the mug and throws it into the trash. He blows on the tea again and then takes a sip.

He walks back over to the drawer to the right of the silverware, opens it, and takes the garlic grinder out. He puts it on the counter. He walks across the room and opens a drawer across the room, and takes out two pill containers. He opens them and places the plastic caps on the countertop in a row. He takes two pills from one, one from the other, and puts them in the garlic grinder, in place of a garlic clove, and he smashes them up. Not much of it came through the other end, and he had to use a butter knife and then a fork to get the crushed pill out, and he does, and he gets it all into the bowl of grits that's been cooling on the counter, and he stirs it together.

He adds butter and a splash of the milk to the grits and pills, and continues to stir as he stares into the other room at the home shopping channel that's still on the television screen. He takes a bite of the grits, then another, and another.

He puts the spoon down, and picks up the pencil again and starts doodling, just drawing lines, on the paper in front of him, and there's a creaking of the floor behind him, and it's his mother, Momma Exler, and she walks past him, looks down at his drawing, and says, "Good morning, van Gogh, Freaky." And then he finishes up his grits as she makes her first cup of tea of the day.

Chapter Twenty-five

Shooting at the Store

Now it's now, later that same day, and this is how it is:

Thyme's putting on his hat, his sweatshirt, the same khakis he's had for two or three seasons now; he washes them and waits in his boxers and a t-shirt as they wash and dry and then he'll put them back on. He has his sunglasses in his pocket, they've gotten scratched, and he really only needs them to avoid conversations with people, to avoid eye contact.

And he has his camera with him.

Suzanne asked him to pick up a few things: tea bags, honey, carrots, and soymilk.

He's walking to the store, the one where he used to work. He figures that today is Erin's day to be on shift; he waits until her shift should be starting.

He can't seem to find anything he wants to take pictures of; the ones he does shoot don't turn out well. He's thinking he should have left the camera at home.

He takes the last turn and there's the store, a block and a half away. Two boys are sitting at the far end of the parking lot, each with two drumsticks and an upturned empty bucket. They look twelve years old; one black, one white; both with baseball hats on. They're looking down, beating on their buckets; Thyme finds himself waiting to see either a bucket crack or a drumstick break, but they don't, nothing breaks and the boys keep on drumming and drumming. He raises his camera and walks closer and takes a shot, tries another, moves to the other side, kneels down on one knee and takes some more photos. This feels right to him. He's enjoying it. He takes some more and the boys finally notice him; they stop playing, they start to make funny faces at the camera, one gives the other bunny ears, Thyme clicks one more, reaches into his pocket and puts a dollar into each hat that they've taken off their heads and held towards him.

He turns, walks towards the entrance of the store, he hears, "One, Two, Three, Four" and click clack click clack the wooden drumsticks hit the empty plastic buckets with a raging excitement. He walks slowly to the store; he knows that once inside the overhead speakers and the constant beeps of the registers will overpower the drumming outside. It's been a while since he worked a shift here.

He finds the tea aisle; he knows exactly where everything is. He grabs some tea, two kinds, one he sees Momma drink every morning, and one kind he'd seen before and wants to try. Next he grabs some organic carrots. Then he walks to the milk, it takes him a minute to remember where the soymilk is, all the way to the left, at the bottom.

He forgets about the honey. He doesn't even know he forgot something; sometimes he'll have to wander around the aisles, know he was looking for six things and he's only got five; so he has to wander around, is he looking for paper towels, avocados, sugar? But today, he looks at his tea, two boxes, carrots, and milk, and smiles and says to himself, Good job.

He walks to the self checkout and scans his groceries, puts them all in a paper bag, pays in cash, sticking the bills into the machine and he takes his change but he forgets his receipt.

He looks around the store; no one he wants to talk to or have eye contact with; he feels for his sunglasses in his pocket. Thyme walks over to the office, the door is open, and the light is on. Erin is sitting behind the desk, casually looking through the day's mail. He knocks twice on the door frame, she looks up, puts down the mail, and says, "Well, Thyme, come on in. How are you? How's the hand?"

He takes a few steps in, doesn't sit down, and he smiles and says, "It was better before someone shot me," and he smiles, Erin does too. She then yawns, rubs her eyes.

Thyme says, "You look tired; you been working too late?"

"Not really working; just going out late with this guy I met. He's keeping me up late, and waking me up early."

Thyme smiles and holds up his hand, "Too much information, Erin, too much information. Anyway, I need to get walking back; Mom needs the carrots to cook with."

"You need a ride?"

"Aren't you on the clock right now?"

"I guess . . . but I'm not really busy."

"Neither am I. Thanks, but no thanks. I'll walk. I'll see you later."

"Tell Momma 'hello' for me."

Thyme nods, walks out the office door, through the automatic doors that open in front of him, and out into the parking lot, where he sees the kids are no longer banging their buckets.

And he hadn't taken more than fifteen steps when he landed his calloused toes down on an uncommonly sharp rock. He's jolted out of his daze, and his toes hurt; he puts the bag down on the trunk of the blue car he happens to be walking past, and he bends down to inspect his throbbing foot.

No blood.

Just cold fire.

And that's when the hair on the back of his neck stood up, but not from pain; from something else.

His heart skipped, like it did once or twice when he did too much junk years ago, back when he was just a bearded skinny skeleton in a ripped shirt.

His eyes look left and right making sure no cars are coming; he's hunched over, nursing his hurt toes, wiping off dirt. His right knee was almost knocking into that rectangular scar on the bumper of the car, that car, this car, the blue one that was in the driveway, that driveway.

He puts both feet on the ground.

He turns towards the car, and stares at the yin and yang sticker. He looks to the bag on the trunk, on the trunk of the blue car, looks at the insignia above the license plate.

All of a sudden he can taste painkillers in his mouth, on the back of his tongue, going into his throat, he can taste phantom painkillers. Or at least the painkillers from two hours ago.

He keeps his paper bag on the trunk of the car. And then he remembers. He remembers.

Honey.

Suzanne didn't need the carrots to cook with tonight, those were for tomorrow, she needed honey, that was the most important thing that she needed, and he forgot.

So he stares at the blue car for a minute and grabs his paper bag, and turns back to the store.

He needs honey.

The blue car is here; he remembers the picture he took, with the image up near the dormer window, he remembers the man, face down dead, and he remembers later knocking on the door when no one answered. And now he needs honey. He's happy he's a little stoned still, happy to have the taste of the painkillers in his mouth, maybe they'll go back into his blood stream again. He hopes so.

He walks directly to the honey, he knows the fastest route, he knows what brand is to the left and what brand is to the right, and he grabs the one in the middle.

He's on the honey aisle, the one with the jams, the jellies, and the preserves. He walks past the next aisle and looks to his left, up the aisle, and there's a woman with her back turned, slender, longer dark hair, a blue bag with her, and then she walks off.

He pauses.

Is it?

He keeps going and looks down the next aisle, and there are two women, also both slender, both with hair past their shoulders, one has what Thyme would call a dark light-blue bag and the other what he would call a light dark-blue bag, both looking away from him.

He pauses again. Then he starts walking again.

Past the next aisle: it's empty.

The next aisle has a woman in it, her back turned towards him, long brownish hair, he likes her shape, she's got a blue bag, but then she leaves the aisle from the far end and she's gone.

He walks on; he's almost to the self checkout center.

He looks down the next aisle. It's empty.

Then he looks down the next aisle, and he sees Erin on that aisle, with a clipboard and some mail, and she's looking perkier now. She talking to a man, she's flirting with a man, Thyme can see, and the man's looking into Erin's eyes and then openly eyeing her up and down, laughing with her.

And then the man shifts his weight from one leg to another and Thyme pays more attention to the man than he had a moment ago, and sees a bandage on his ear, notices the smaller one on his nose, the swelling.

The taste of painkillers is back.

On his tongue.

Way back on his tongue.

That acidic taste is back.

He increases his step and stuffs his left hand, his hurt hand, into his pocket a little too quickly, and jams it, and winces in pain.

It's him, he thinks to himself. It's him and I don't want to get into this now, he thinks.

He reaches into his pocket, the pocket of his sweatshirt and not too hard this time, not too hard as to hurt his hand, and he pulls out his sunglasses, the scratched ones, and puts them on. His defense.

He goes up to the self check out aisles; there are four of them. Two of the aisles are women with long brownish hair, both taking cash out of their blue bags to pay for their groceries.

Thyme looks back at the aisle he's just passed; he hears Erin laughing. He doesn't scan his customer card he just buys the honey and stuffs a five dollar bill into the slot and takes the receipt but he forgets his change and he throws the honey into a bag and he walks to the blue car in the parking lot and he grabs his bag of groceries. He walks home as fast as he can, his camera hitting against his chest with each step, bouncing in stride with his steps, hitting his left side, then his right side, then his left.

Back in the store, Stan never saw Thyme.

He left Erin on the greeting card aisle. They were going out again tomorrow night. He walked down to the end of the aisle, turned to the left, and came down the next row.

There is only one customer on this aisle, with her long hair, her blue bag: Chastity.

Stan walks slower, passes behind her, takes a deep whiff of air, tries to smell her, all of her, any of her. He gets his cell phone out of his pocket; he holds it so he's not covering the lens. He loves his cell phone. He aims it at her backside as he passes. He takes another deep breath.

She pretends not to notice.

She picks up a bag of sugar, holds it against her hip, and walks towards the bags of flour.

He passes her, pretends to look at whole wheat flour, and turns to her, worried about his left nostril might start to bleed, and he smiles.

"You finished that book yet?"

Chastity looks at Stan, doesn't smile, and says, "No."

Stan looks down at Chastity's bag, and then says to her, "You got it in that bag?" His cell phone is aimed at her chest, goes down to her legs, up to her neck.

"Maybe."

"You know, I once met Suzanne Exler; I even got my picture with her. I should send them to you. You'd enjoy them."

She looks blankly at him.

He continues, "What's your email address? I'll send you some pictures of me with her. Put them in your blog, if you have a one."

"I don't have email right now."

"Oh. Too bad."

"But I think I shot her son once, though, not too long ago."

Stan couldn't stop himself from starting to smile; his left nostril started to bleed, again.

"You shot Suzanne Exler's son?"

Chastity says nothing; nods in the affirmative.

"Come on, I'm going to buy your groceries today. When you get up there tell Erin to put your food on my card, she's got it."

The he walks off, smiling, bleeding from his left nostril, and laughing, 'Suzanne's demented punk kid got shot; I already feel better.'

Chastity, on the other hand, sticks a jar of Vaseline and a tube of toothpaste in her blue bag before allowing Stan to buy the rest of her groceries for her. 'I'm a virgin, not an angel.' And she smiled and stood in line and thought about dinner, and the old lady in line in front of her, and she looked at the glossy magazines with celebrity affairs, and she looked at the paper tabloids with aliens predicting earthquakes, and she thought about a lot of things, but not about Stan Thimble.

Thyme's been walking for maybe ten minutes. He's thinking about smoking, about getting high. It's what he's always thinking about. He's thinking about stirring some smashed painkillers into some tea and smoking some pot.

And then the car passes him; the blue one.

This is a neighborhood road, so the speed limit is slow and the blue car is doing less than that, so Thyme has time to put his paper bag of groceries down on the sidewalk, lift up his camera, and take a couple shots of the rear of the car driving away from him, the missing sticker to the left, the circle to the right.

He gets home, opens the door, Suzanne's not home, he goes into the kitchen and gets a Percocet and pulls his pipe from his pocket, then a bag of the pot, and packs it. He gets a penny from his pocket, from the change from the groceries, and he uses it to crush the Percocet on the table, and he picks up the pieces and pours it over the green herb in his glass pipe and steps out the back door, and holds a lighter up with his good hand, his right one, and smokes a few minutes and by then the grocery store feels like yesterday and the blue car was just a coincidence and it's time to just stare at the fallen leaves for a while, watch the sun go down, and just think about nothing.

He empties his pocket of change, and three pennies roll around the counter, down onto the floor, and under the refrigerator.

Stan Thimble, on the other hand, thought a lot about one thing, Chastity. On the way home, he found himself driving and thinking about nothing but her. He speeds; ten miles over the limit, twelve miles.

He gets home, doesn't put up his car windows or lock the doors. He goes into his house, locks the deadbolt behind him, goes to his computer, and turns it on. While it boots up, he takes off his belt. He types in his password in a hurry. He connects his cell phone to his computer, doesn't bother with closing the blinds or curtains, and he stares at the images of Chastity in the store, he stares for an hour at the images of Chastity over a screensaver of Suzanne in the supply room.

Stan had never been to Erin's house before; she had been over to his, but he did not even have her address.

Later that night, he sat in the parking lot across from the store, and when Erin walked out and went to her car, he slowly followed her home. He watched her park her car. He turned on his cell phone, and held it up, and took pictures of Erin unlocking her door, and walking in, and then he watches a minute, then two, and another light turns on, and he sees Erin walk over to the window, and he takes a picture of this, and she closes the blinds, and then Stan is sure that's her bedroom.

Chapter Twenty-six

Unemployment, Photographs, and Home Remedy Painkillers

Now it's now, the next morning, and this is how it is:

Thyme's awake. He's in the kitchen, hunched over the sink with an empty coffee cup in his good hand, and he's watching the steam rise out of the sink. It takes longer to steam up now, in the fall, with the pipes under the old house getting cold at night. He finally lifts the empty coffee mug to the water and fills it. He turns the water off, places the mug on the counter, and tosses a tea bag in. Then he opens the microwave, places the mug inside, hits one minute and twelve seconds, slams the door shut, hits Start, and he stares into the microwave.

He already smells like pot. His fingers stink of it.

He takes the mug out, stirs it, blows on it, and extracts his tea bag, then throws in parts of two smashed painkillers.

He stirs the tea again, stares out the kitchen window for three minutes, maybe four, then blows on the tea and takes a taste. The tea takes away the painkiller's taste; he likes tea. He takes a second sip, then a third. It's time to smoke again. Tea and herbs, those are his home remedies; he smiles about that, he smiles thinking about his photographs, his unemployment, and his painkillers.

He doesn't have to worry about money too much: Suzanne doesn't make him pay rent or part of the bills, he doesn't drive, doesn't even have a license right now, so he doesn't care whether barrels of oil are trading for $50 or $150. He doesn't ever eat out; he knows how to throw a meal together.

Now it's getting to be near the end of the homegrown weed, maybe another weeks' worth, maybe less; it was worth it while it lasted, and, he thought, when he runs out he'll be able to actually read a book and not lose interest after reading one page two times. And he only had a few days left worth of pain pills; though he was sure he had some leftover in another old

116

container somewhere in the kitchen or maybe in the computer room. He wasn't smiling, knowing that in a few days he'd be out his home remedy painkillers and left only with photography and unemployment.

He cocks his ears and listens for those ghostly dog tags jingling, but he doesn't hear them. So, stoned, he walks over to the front door, opens it and whistles, but he doesn't hear anything, but a woman jogging by looks at him, scowls, flicks him off, and then jogs on.

Thyme shakes his head and whistles again, saying, "Here, boy."

It's starting out as a gray morning. It hasn't actually rained today, just some haze, some small water drips just hanging in the air.

Suzanne is drinking her tea.

She's been busy recently, driving around from here to there, and driving fast to one thing and then she'll jump into her car, zoom off, past the policeman on the corner, the one who's watched her speed by him for years and years and never stopped her.

She's volunteering with a homeless shelter; she works in the clothes closest, she works in the kitchen, she sits in the big room with all the cots and just talks to people. She hands out dollar bills to people, from her own account.

She figures she's ok; she may be out of a job, but she's ok. She has the house. She's paid that off a few years ago, ahead of time. She has some stocks, even though they were worth more a few years ago. Some government bonds. She keeps her cash in three banks.

And then she's off to see some developer; she's writing a piece on a building renovation for a local monthly print magazine. She was hoping to get this all done on a sunny day; Suzanne likes her dreary days to herself; she likes to turn up the radio and speed alone, faster on turns, on days like this.

Her tea's done. She's done watching the cable news; it's started to repeat itself. She finished her hemp bran blueberry muffin. She throws a paperback into the bag she's taking with her; she never leaves home without a book.

She's a little nervous, a little anxious.

She can't tell if it's because she took some of Thyme's pills last night to make her sleep better and this is residual, but she swears that as she's been blowing on her tea that Stan Thimble drove by in his car.

She talks to Thyme, at the far end of the room, alternating between drawing on a legal pad and staring out the front windows. Now, he's in the staring part; the pencil hovering above the paper.

"Thyme?"

"Yes, Momma?" He doesn't look her direction.

"Did you see that car that went by? Twice?"

"The red one?"

"The red one."

"That's the third time it went by Momma; I was outside earlier and saw it."

Suzanne nods, "I think it's that demented toe-rag's car. You know the one."

"I know the one, Momma."

She thinks about the can of pepper spray in her bag; she thinks about setting those photos on fire.

She looks down at her shoes; she thinks about kicking Stan Thimble.

She takes her mug of tea to the sink, turns on the cold water and fills it, then turns off the water, and turns around.

"Well, Thyme, I guess I should get going."

"I'll walk out with you."

"No, no. I'll be ok." She smiles over at Thyme, who is still not looking at her but now drawing, and she says, "Have a good morning, van Gogh, sweetie."

"Don't worry, Momma."

"What's that, Thyme?"

"Don't worry, Momma, he'll get his, one day."

She looks at him, nods, and then she's out the door and on the sidewalk and looks both ways and doesn't see the red car anywhere and she gets in her car, turns on the engine, and takes off as fast as she can, with her tires squealing.

Stan had driven by; he'd driven by more often than Suzanne knew about, although Thyme realizes now that he did recognize the car and that he had seen it more than he told Suzanne about. He just never knew whose car it was; until now.

Stan drives by and looks at the windows of Suzanne's house; he wishes he could drive by and see the kitchen counter through the windows, but that's in the back of the house. He takes photos of the house with his cell phone. He's at the point where he thinks nothing about it; he'll drive by five times in one day and point and click and drive off. He loves those sights, those photos of Suzanne in her kitchen, Erin in his, and of Chastity (although he doesn't know her name).

He decides to drive by one more time; he doesn't know that Suzanne has just sped off the other direction. He turns the car around, and heads back to pass by the Exler house one more time.

As soon as Suzanne left, Thyme went out back to light up the pipe, and he sucked it through real fast, stuck the piece in his pocket, and walked around the side of the house. He's watching where he steps; he's barefoot, of course. Barefoot in the midst of sharp rocks, he sees one glimmer, like fools gold, so he stops and picks it up and keeps on going.

He's still in their yard, but walking up the side property line towards the front, when he sees the red car drive up, and slow down. Thyme picks up his speed. He's almost running towards the car but hasn't said anything.

Stan's reaching his arm out of his red car, he'd seen Suzanne's car was gone, and he assumed that the coast was clear. Thyme, a good shot from throwing tennis balls recently, threw a speedball with the rock towards the extended hand, hits it dead on, and the cell phone falls to the ground.

Stan's hand goes back inside the car and he's opening the door again and has his foot on the ground when Thyme runs up and grabs the door and slams it onto Stan's ankle. Thyme then kicks the door one more time for good measure, and he spits at Stan as Stan is flooring the accelerator and speeding away.

Thyme reaches down and picks up the cell phone, puts it in his pocket, the one without the pipe. He stops.

He's forgotten his camera.

He goes back inside, puts Stan's cell phone down on the table, grabs his own camera and hangs it around his neck, makes sure the back door is locked, then walks out the front door and locks it after him.

Now he's off for his daily walk.

It takes him about fifteen 15 minutes to get to Chastity's neighborhood. He sees more For Sale signs than he did just the other day; when he gets there, Chastity's yard still needs to be raked.

He sits in the yard across the street. Chastity's house is the only one that looks like it has any signs of life. A kitchen light is on. Thyme has his camera in his hand. A television is on inside. Thyme takes off the lens cap. The upstairs bedroom light is going on and off, then nothing for thirty seconds, then on and off, then nothing, then on and off. He takes a picture of the house with the light off. Thirty seconds pass and it comes back on. He takes another picture. Thirty seconds pass and it goes off. He takes a final picture and takes his finger off the camera trigger. It comes back on. Then goes off again. Then it comes back on and stays. Thyme sees someone walk over to the window, and look out. Thyme can see her well. He can see her brown hair, her shoulders.

He lifts the camera again, zooms in on her, she's looking right into the lens, he takes a shot, then another. She just stares at him. She doesn't smile, she doesn't smirk, she doesn't snarl, she just stares.

Then she turns around. She walks away from the window, and turns the light off. Thyme doesn't see her again. He sits for five minutes, he thinks of making ants on a log with some broken pills instead of raisins, and he gets up, stares a little longer at the house, and walks back home for a painkiller snack.

When he gets home, there's a voice mail from Momma, he plays it, and she says she's going to be out later than she thought, work a little later, and maybe drive around after that. She says what he can set out to thaw for his dinner tonight, and then kisses, she says, she'll see him in the morning, she'll cover him if he's asleep on the sofa in front of the television.

He hangs up the phone. He walks over the refrigerator and hunts around for the celery, then Momma's dairy free cream cheese, grabs a butter knife and put it all down on the cutting board. He takes out his prescription bottle from where he left it in the spice rack, next to the cumin, takes out a couple pills, breaks them in half, then halves those, and sticks them into the cream cheese he's put on the celery.

He's swallowed one bite, he's chewing the second one, when he remembers the cell phone that Stan dropped. He walks over to it, holds it in his bad hand and starts pressing buttons on it with his right hand, finds the photos section, scans through a few and says, "Why am I not surprised?"

He scans through photos of Momma: in the kitchen, right there on that counter, and in some office, it's her; and then he sees Erin. He brings the little image closer to his blue eyes, he's never seen Erin like this, and there are photos of this house, there are at least two dozen of them, in some of them Suzanne's car is out front, in one the leaves are raked, in another they need to be raked, one is in the rain, one at night, one in the day, one shows Thyme just sitting on the steps of the house looking up at the clouds. Then there are some photos from what looks to be the grocery store Erin works at, and there's a photo of a woman with a blue bag, and then he sees in another picture that it's her, it's the woman who was on the roof the night he took those photos.

He goes back to the images of Erin. He zooms in a little; yep, it's her.

He takes another crunch of his pain concoction. He chews on it for a while.

Thyme sticks the cell phone in his pocket, lifts his camera back up and puts it around his neck, grabs his baseball hat and walks out the door, again making sure he locks it behind him.

Erin's working now, he says, to himself, and he takes off walking to the store to talk to Erin, show her what Stan Thimble has in his cell phone.

Now it's now, later that night, and this is how it is: It's raining and the roads are all wet, and headlights reflect off the city streets.

Stan Thimble is limping when he walks in the bar to meet Erin; his shin was bleeding, and is now bruised and scabbed. He had gotten home, after his encounter with Thyme, from losing his cell phone, and he pulled out the blender and made himself a smoothie and tossed in three pills before he pushed the High button. He drank it as he sat on the sofa, and he drank it down with his eyes closed and he thought about Erin the way she was the other night, in his bed. He finished the drink and felt good and he sat on the sofa thinking about Erin, and Suzanne, and he felt good, and then it was time for him to get up and go.

The pain-pill-smoothie was starting to wear off as he walked in and sat on a barstool next to Erin, who was smoking a cigarette.

She was drinking a bottled beer.

He sat down and smiled at her, hadn't even said Hello before Erin puts her cigarette cherry down into the top of his hand with her left hand, it's sizzling; then she upturns her beer, finishes it off, stands up as she's doing it, still holding the cigarette into Stan's flesh, and with her right hand she hits Stan in the nose with the empty beer bottle; both nostrils start bleeding.

She lets go of the cigarette, puts the bottle down calmly, and says to Stan, "I already feel better."

He reaches out and grabs her hand quickly, and says to her, "I think you'll see me again," and she slips away and leaves the bar.

Stan leaves the bar and gets in his car, stops by a liquor store, nose bleeding on the rum aisle. He goes home, swallows two pills, crushing one with his molars, and drinks, watching television, holding a handkerchief up to his nose, especially the bloody left side.

Now it's now, later that night, and this is how it ended:

Thyme's asleep, Stan's asleep, and Chastity's asleep.

Suzanne is driving quickly on the slick roads, and she puts her car into an old oak tree when she misses a curve, it's dark and late, she's alone, and she's up against the windshield (just like Wylde).

The telephone wakes Thyme early in the morning, or in the middle of the night, either one. He finds shoes, for the first time in a long while, and he sits and puts them on, and ties them, listening to the silent house. He leaves through the front door, locks it behind him, and starts walking to the hospital, to identify her; he sucks on a pill like a mint as he walks alone, crying.

He doesn't hear a collar jingle today.

Part Four

As Momma Lay Dying, Three Pennies, & Other Daydreams

Chapter Twenty-seven

A Funeral with Empty Prescriptions

It's a couple of days later, now, and this is how it is:
As Momma lay dying?
No.
Not at all.
Momma never lay dying; she just died in a flash, just like that.

As Thyme lay dying?
Yes.
More like that.
Thyme lay dying; thinking of Momma, dying in a flash, just like that.

Thyme ran out painkillers the day after he identified Momma in the hospital morgue.

He sucked on one on the way like a bitter mint, walking to the hospital in his walking shoes, the ones he hasn't worn in forever, without socks. He sat in the waiting room a while, sucking on a pill; he bummed a cigarette, walked back outside and smoked it, and then went to the morgue.

On the way home, he bummed another cigarette, smoked half of it, gagged, threw the cigarette on the ground, and threw up on the road.

He walked home, unlocked the front door, left it wide open, grabbed the bottle of painkillers, and dumped the last two from the container onto the counter top.

He's wearing his corduroys and has three pennies in his pocket; he'd been rubbing the pennies together when he was in the waiting room, and then outside smoking, and then in the morgue, and on the way home. He took one of the pennies and smashed both pills on the countertop and he puts his nose on the pile and snorts as hard as he can and then he licks the remainder of the bitter white-yellow pile, gags, and cries.

Then he sits on the front steps, looking to where Suzanne's car would have been, if it didn't end up in an oak tree, in the dark, in the rain. He has the rest of his marijuana with him; he rolls a joint with all that he has left; he sits there and smokes it slowly while joggers jogged by; he sat there smoking it as a red car slowed down as it passed; and he sat there smoking his joint, staring up into the sky, focusing on nothing; he sits there smoking and he cries, with tears falling down onto his shoes.

He hears a whimper from down next to his dirty shoes.

He sleeps in those shoes that night, when he falls asleep before dusk, on the sofa, in front of the television.

He woke up at midnight, stumbled around, heard creaks in the house, felt in his pocket for his pipe, hit it empty, got a little smoke from the black tar inside, and shuffled down the hallway to his bedroom.

He slept all the next day, waking at dinner, to call Erin at the store, who knew about Suzanne's death, she'd seen the obits. She told Thyme she'd pick him up and take him to the funeral the next day. He stretches and closes his eyes, and thinks he hears creaks in the hallway, her footsteps, and he thinks he hears Momma's voice in the kitchen, and he thinks he can smell her tea in the air. He opens his eyes; he can't get any rest recently.

He checks here and there for pills he may have squirreled away, but finds nothing.

He pulls the glass pipe from his pocket, he's still wearing the same pants, and shirt, and shoes as last night, or yesterday afternoon, whichever. He finds a pocket knife, three paper clips, two jumbo and one regular, and grabs a piece of paper, folds it in half, and begins to prod the pipe with the paper clips. Within minutes, his fingers are black and pungent; there is a pile of black goo on the paper, and he rolls it into a ball, and sticks it into the pipe.

He walks out the front door; he closes it but doesn't lock it behind him.

He walks down the street, it's basically dark, and he's walking in his shoed feet, and holding the lighter to the bowl every minute or so and holding his breath for a minute and then exhaling and then doing it again. It turns gray. It's done.

He wants to smash the pipe all of a sudden, so he takes it and throws it down on the street as hard as he can, and nothing happens. He smashes his heel onto the pipe but ends up only hurting his leg. It never breaks. He throws it as hard as he can, he hears it hit the street, and still not break.

He keeps walking.

Thyme says to himself: "That's all. No more painkillers."

He walks up to where the bowl lay in the road, and he kicks it, and it shatters.

This is the same day, and this is how it is:

Chastity stole a newspaper from a house on the next block (she's a virgin, not an angel), and was flipping through the obituaries, when she saw 'Exler, Suzanne'. The obituary said she was in her mid-sixties, and was survived by a son, Thymothy X Exler.

She saw when the funeral was, and found her black dress and ironed it, even though she hadn't done that in years, and went to bed early, on the sofa, watching the news.

Now Momma's dead, and Thyme has written a eulogy just for her: Suzanne Exler, Momma Thyme, was a rolling stone that rolled and rolled and rolled, but gathered no moss, and will one day sooner be turning to dust. Momma was a jazz record, she was that trumpet, you know the one; she was the blood running through the drummer's veins, she was the sweat on the piano keys, the beating kick drum; she was that high hat cymbal that went crash and she burned on the inside and she yearned on the inside and she was a jazz, a jazz that's not so stoned-like, a jazz record, that jazz joint being smoked in the middle of a joke, no broken jazz, all burning jazz: Momma was a jazz that wasn't so stoned, no scratches, no skips: just solos, and you know it meant a thing, because Momma had that swing.

Suzanne had her funeral arranged in advance; there was nothing much for Thyme to do but kill time.

He found a shirt and some blacks pants that didn't look too bad, and thought about shaving but changed his mind, looked again for some pills to no avail, found a tie, and tied it around his neck. He had to untie it two or three times until he finally got it right; it had been years since he'd last tied a tie.

He'd been wearing and sleeping in those khakis for days. He could still smell the morgue in the legs, the hospital antiseptic smell clung to his hands; he hasn't showered, and his hands still smell like the cigarettes he bummed.

He takes off the khakis, doing it the hard way, keeping his walking shoes on and pulling and tugging and yanking the pants over the shoes, and then pulling the black pants up over them, still sockless. He pulls the belt out of the khakis and remembers when he and Maria would use the belt to tie up and shoot up; he can't believe that Maria just popped into his head. She had brown eyes, but that was years ago.

Erin pulls up out front, also dressed in her best black, and she parks, walks to the door, knocks gently, and hugs Thyme when he opens the door; he starts to cry again.

Now it's now, and this is how it is:

Stan Thimble, whose left nostril has finally stopped bleeding, has not found a job and he has not run out of pain killers, either; he went to the doc in a box and got a new prescription, all the while trying to get the nurse's phone number. But now he sits at his kitchen table, he takes two pills and crushes them, gets a banana, unpeels it, and rolls it around in the pile of crushed pills, and then proceeds to eat it as he drinks his coffee and unrolls the newspaper. It's an older paper; from a day or two ago; he causally flips through the Metro section, and as he turns to the obituaries, his eyes focus on Suzanne's picture, and he chokes a bit on his coffee, spits some on the floor after some started coming back out of his nose, burning his nose, and he reads it two, three times, and then cries. He loathed her, he might have loved her, and how he wanted her.

He finishes his pill encrusted banana, and wishes he still had his cell phone. He pours another cup of coffee and goes to take a shower, where he cries some more. When he comes out and dries off, he feels that warm feeling starting in his stomach.

He starts to get dressed for the funeral; he's not going to the service, he's decided that's too risky, he may run into some of the twits he used to work with, or Suzanne's crazy parasitic son.

Chastity's driving there, to the grave side, after skipping the service at the funeral home.

Thyme, too, skips the service; he couldn't bear to go; he stands at the grave, that deep open pit, and rubs three pennies together in his pocket, while Erin, really his only friend, holds his hand to try to comfort him. The ground is cold; he imagines his mother shivering in her casket, yelling out that she's not dead, that she's not ready to go, but she's dead all right, and he knows it. He saw a picture of the car, headfirst into the tree, that the insurance company took, and he knew it was a fast death, face first into the spider webbed glass, the glass breaking her neck.

Ashes to ashes.

Dust to dust.

Eyes are tearing up behind his scratched sunglasses, the ones he used to wear to hide his narcotic dazed eyes.

Ashes to ashes, dust to dust, and before he knows it, it's all over; it seems to last all day, but it also seems to have just started. Erin held his hand and she was crying the whole time, too.

And then comes the real blitz, the real confusion: people are coming up and hugging him, shaking his hand, putting their hands on his shoulders, talking about Suzanne, his Momma, and he can hardly hear them, he cannot respond, he'd break down and become ashes to ashes and dust to dust himself.

He nods and he tries to smile; he lets the tears run down his cheek into his beard.

And that's when Erin starts clutching his hand so hard that he feels a crack of bone; it's his hurt hand, his bad hand; and still Erin doesn't let go; he glances at her through the dark scratched lenses of his sunglasses and can see that something's wrong; she's staring over towards one of the old parts of the cemetery, thirty yards away.

Thyme sees what she's looking at.

A man.

The one in the dark suit, leaning up against a tall monument, he knows him.

He drops her hand.

He walks away mid-sentence from a woman giving him her condolences, and he starts walking away from Momma's grave site, from Momma in her casket, and both of his hands are in fists, and he starts to increase his pace.

Thyme never says a thing: he's running now in his walking shows, sockless, with his fists out. Stan, also not saying a thing, does not recognize Thyme until he's too close, and Stan's first instinct is to smile, which seems like a bad idea a split second later, and then he instinctively raises his hands to protect his bandaged nose, and that's the same time that Thyme's right fist makes contact with Stan's hands held up in front of his nose, and Thyme's fist and both of Stan's hands are thrust into Stan's broken nose, and he screams, and before he's fallen onto his back, the bandage that was white when he got out of his car is turning red. Stan's on his back, between two graves, saying, "No, no", and then Thyme kicks him in his groin, and spits onto Stan's face, and then raises his left foot over Stan's face and says, "Go away before I crush your nose, again."

Stan tries to get up, falls, tries again successfully and then he walks towards his car as fast as he can. He takes a look to his left and sees Thyme slowly following him. To his right he sees some of the people he used to work with at the online magazine, looking over at him, shaking their heads, and avoiding eye contact.

Thyme watches Stan walk off, hunched over a little from pain, holding his left nostril, and he gets in his car, flips Thyme the middle finger, and then drives off, tires tossing rocks from the gravel road in the cemetery.

Thyme already feels better, feels good.

He's walking back to the graveside, where Erin is waiting for him, and a woman walks up to him seemingly from out of nowhere; she's been hiding behind one of the graves, the hiding girl, and he recognizes her; she says, "I'm sorry. I'm sorry about your mother. I'm sorry I shot you."

All he can do right now is say "Yeah" and more tears roll into his beard and then she turns and walks off, and he walks towards Erin, without stopping, and he says, "Please take me home now."

Erin makes sure that Stan's car is out of the cemetery before she goes up to her car, opens the passenger side door for Thyme, and then walks around to the driver's side and gets in.

She turns on the car, and looks in the mirror as the car warms up, and she sees Chastity, behind them, watching, watching Erin and Thyme sit in the car.

Erin looks over at Thyme, "Are you alright?"

He nods.

"Are you sure?"

"I'll be okay, soon."

She starts to drive, slowly, and then says to him, "Stan scares me."

"Me, too."

"I've had dreams at night about him, bad dreams."

He nods, "Me, too."

Chapter Twenty-eight

A Fall on the Stairs

This is an hour later, now, and this is how it is:

Chastity pulls her car into the driveway, she's been listening to a sports broadcast on the radio, without even knowing it. She turns off the car, tosses the keys into her blue bag, and slams the car door after her. She's hurrying up the sidewalk, feeling a little queasy after the funeral, and her foot slips on the first brick step heading to the front door and she slams down hard on her right side, ribs onto the bricks, and for a second she's out of breath and then her eyes start to water and she sneezes, laying there on the cold brick, she sneezes again and bites her tongue.

After a minute, when she's breathing slower and holding back her tears, she gets up and opens the door and walks in. She tries to kick off her shoes, but decides she needs to lay down on the sofa first; she's feeling light headed, dizzy.

She puts her head down on a pillow; the television has been left on, on mute, and she turns up the volume and puts another pillow over her eyes and falls asleep listening to the news.

This was at the same time, and this how it is:

Stan goes home and stuffs five crushed pills into a blueberry muffin he bought at a local gas station; he eats it as quickly as he can, chasing it with a warm beer. He chomps away; he thinks his front tooth may be loose. He thinks about his pills; he's in a lot of pain; he's going to need more.

He thinks he should take a nap first, maybe he'll feel better then. He lies on the sofa, putting his head flat on the cushion, and covers his eyes with a pillow. With his eyes closed, he feels for the remote control on the floor, finds it and turns it on, lowering the volume just enough to hear it. He lays with his eyes closed under the pillow, listening to the news, but he cannot fall asleep.

Now, she's getting up.

She steps on the remote by accident and turns off the TV and one of the batteries falls out; she leaves it next to the remote on the floor. She feels her ribs, not too hard, and she winces in pain. Her side is red and a little blue, but not bleeding, now.

She goes up to the library. She opens the desk drawer; she rolls herself a painkiller.

It's an hour or so later, now, and she's getting into her car, and sits there for a few minutes before turning it on; she's afraid she's broken a rib. She takes a deep breath and it hurts.

She turns the car on and starts to drive towards the hospital, the same one Thyme walked to just days ago. She finds a parking spot; she wonders if the insurance card that she has is any good. She got the card from the man she was living with, the one who died up on the roof, or died on the driveway, or maybe died somewhere in between.

She walks thru the front doors; they open automatically and the cold air is replaced by a warm smell of sanitizers. She finds the front desk, asks where she should go, and walks down a hallway, thru some other doors, and finds a second desk with two nurses. One hands her a clipboard but not a pen. Chastity finds a seat, it's next to one man but there's no one to her right.

She holds the clipboard in front of her, staring at the questions. She chews on the top of a pen she found in her blue bag. She starts filling out the first page, Last Name, First Name, Middle Initial, Date of Birth, and the man to her left gets up after a name is called and at the same time another man sits down on her right. She continues: Street Number, Street Name, Zip Code, Daytime Phone, Nighttime Phone, her elbow accidently nudges the man to her right, the one that had sat there a minute ago, and she continues, Emergency Contact, and then she stops. She can't think of anyone to write down for an Emergency Contact.

She just looking at the blank line in front of her, and that's when she gets the feeling that she's being watched, and out of her peripheral vision, to her right, she sees the man next to her is looking at her clipboard, at her name, her address, at the blank line next to her Emergency Contact, and she recognizes the swollen nose, the blood stain under the left nostril, and Stan smiles at her, after looking up from her clipboard, and all of a sudden she gets light headed, her vision gets dim, and she turns and vomits into his lap and then slumps down onto the floor.

The nurses behind the desk, pens in hand, hurry across the room, ignoring Stan and pushing him out of the way as he's covered in vomit.

She wakes up, still in her clothes but covered under a white blanket in a new room. She closes her eyes again and remembers being in the rows of tombstones earlier today, and falls into a dream of her as a child, lost among marble tombstones.

There she was, four years old, in her favorite corduroy pants, with those three pennies in her right pocket, rubbing them together furiously, and lost. Lost. She was wandering among fake flowers and moss growing up on the taller, older headstones. She could hear her foster father calling her name, but he seemed to be far away and little Chastity could not see him and the cemetery seemed huge and all those alabaster angels and cracked crosses above her seemed to stare at her, and she could hear her name being called over and over and now it seems to be getting farther away.

Suddenly, she realizes there is only one penny left in her pocket. She can't remember taking out the other pennies and there's no hole. Little Chastity turns around, walking farther from where her foster father is, and she's got her eyes set on the ground, looking for her lost pennies, she's clutching the remaining penny, warm compared to the air on her cheeks; there are tears falling from her eyes. She's running, her little legs moving as fast as they can.

Then she stops and sees a piece of paper in the grass; she bends down and picks it up with her left hand, the penniless hand, and she turns it over and she, little Chastity, is looking at the same piece of paper she drew of herself and her foster dad in the same cemetery, only, now, the foster father is wearing a bandage over his nose, and his left nostril is colored red, outside the lines as a panic stricken child might color, blood red.

She hears her foster father's voice calling her. Getting farther away. And then little Chastity looks up and she sees Stan, bandaged and bleeding, standing next to a headstone that says Exler, and he's smiling at her and walking towards her, throwing her lost pennies up into the air and catching them and then throwing them again, and when he opens his mouth, it sounds like her foster father, far away, but he's here, right in front of her and getting closer to her. And the last thing she sees is Stan opening his mouth and tossing the two copper coins in and with crazy wide eyes he's shouting at her, she knows he is shouting, but he sounds like her foster father, getting farther away.

Suddenly, Chastity sits up in the hospital, bright lights and beeping machines, artificial warm air, sanitizer fragrance, worried faces, death nearby, neatly folded sheets piled in the corner. She sits up and looks around, then swings her legs to the side of the bed and remembers her ribs, and she lays on her good side and sees a nurse notice her and come over, smiling to her.

This is the same time, now, and this is what Thyme is doing:

He's walking down his front stairs, taking a left, walking sockless in his shoes; it's warmed up a little from this morning; and he's out in shoes, the old pants he'd been wearing more often than not recently, and a long sleeved t-shirt. He has his camera with him, as usual.

He hears that dog tag jingle, and he smiles to himself, he smiles for the first time today.

He gets to the end of the sidewalk; pauses for a minute looking left then right, then left and then right again, trying to decide which way to go. He hears a dog bark to the left and heads that direction.

He walks slowly, aimlessly.

He stops here and there to take some pictures; a photo of an old car with new graffiti, broken doll parts in the middle of the street, one lone mum still blooming in an otherwise dead garden. The farther he walks from his house, Suzanne's house, the more For Sale signs he sees.

He thinks about his shoes as he walks. He doesn't want to think about much at all. His shoes. They feel so weird on his feet.

He sees a woman jog by, about his age, she doesn't make eye contact, just jogs on by; he watches her, he turns as she passes by. He's thinking about sex for the first time in a while.

He keeps going; then he sees something, someone. He stops walking, not quite in the middle of the road and not quite on the side of the road, and he just holds his camera to his eye, and slowly starts to turn in a circle, but slowly, just a little and then just a little more, and he's made a full circle and then is pointed the way he wants to go and he sees through the lens of his camera all of a sudden there is a woman at the end of the block, standing still, with two dogs on leashes.

The dogs are sitting calmly, tongues out, just staring at Thyme; the woman seems to be staring at Thyme as well, through dark sunglasses.

Snap. Snap.

He hears one of those phantom growls he's been hearing recently.

He takes two photos and crosses to the other side of the road; he starts to feel like maybe he shouldn't be where he is; he's on a road he's been on a hundred times, and he feels out of place.

He gets to the other side of the street and continues walking, past a few parked cars, a few For Sale signs; he gets closer to the end of the block and the dogs just continue to stare at him. The woman just stares, too.

And then he's directly across the street from her, and Thyme looks to his left, and the dogs have turned themselves, rearranged themselves, and are looking directly at him.

And then the woman takes off her sunglasses.

She's looking right at Thyme, and he can feel his left knee go weak when all of a sudden he realizes he's staring at a twin of his mother, a twin of Suzanne's, who is staring back at Thyme.

It is Momma.

No.

Momma is dead; under the ground, cold and dead.

It looks like her; but it's not her.

No.

Momma is dead and Thyme is dying from hallucinations.

It's not her; just stop it. Stop it. Stop staring.

Thyme is just staring; he cannot stop. The woman never smiles, but breaks eye contact, and then continues walking. She goes down the street, and she never looks back, and neither do the dogs.

Thyme lifts the camera to his eye and tries to take another picture of the woman and the dogs walking away but something goes wrong with the camera and it won't take the picture. He points it to ground, refocuses it, and it allows him to take a picture, then lifts it up again and tries to take one more frame but it locks up on him. He looks at it, turns an adjustment here and there, and when he looks back up, the woman and the dogs are gone.

Thyme needs to sit down; his left knee is still feeling weak and he's dizzy. He needs to sit down for a minute. He goes into the yard to his left, it looks empty with a weeks' worth of newspapers in their plastic condoms in the driveway and a fallen For Sale sign.

He closes his eyes.

When he opens them, fifteen or twenty minutes later, he realizes that he is diagonally across the street from that house, her house, the girl he saw in the cemetery after Suzanne's funeral, Chastity's house; but the driveway is empty; the blue car is not there.

Thyme is surprised he walked this far without realizing it.

He sits and stares, and then sits and fiddles with his camera; it's working again now.

He gets up, and heads home, taking the long way home; he doesn't want to run into his dead Momma walking those dogs.

He eventually gets home; he opens all the cabinets in the kitchen two or three times and decides he may be a little hungry but not much and he sits on his sofa and stares at the television all night, not really watching it, but not falling asleep either.

Stan is at home later that night; he's got a new prescription and a new bandage and now both sides of his nose won't stop bleeding, and he wishes he had his cell phone, but now he just takes a handful of pills and chews them and he's on the sofa when he falls asleep and then he rolls off onto the floor and hits his nose, but he's had a lot of pain killers, so he sleeps still, and he pisses his pants, and he sleeps through it all, and he won't wake up until morning, when he will awake to a swollen nose, crusty blood, a pounding headache, and pain pills on oatmeal for breakfast.

Chastity's ribs are not broken.

But still, when she breathes it hurts. She sneezed a little while ago and started to cry from the pain; but there's nothing broken.

Chastity drove to a pharmacy and filled the pain prescription. On the way home, she saw some kids on skateboards and she gave the bottle of pills to them (she's a virgin, not an angel).

When she got home, she took a hot shower, and stood there until it got cold. When she got out, she put on only a t-shirt, and found Suzanne Exler's book *Time's Passing;* she tore out a page from the middle, tore that page in half, and rolled it into a joint. She put a jacket on, so she wore only a jacket and a t-shirt, and she climbed out the window from the library, onto the roof of the house, and she sat and she smoked the page from the book, and the pain in her ribs started to subside but she got freaked out about the man with the broken nose in the hospital looking at her name and address on the hospital form. She got freaked out, but just a little; she hit the joint, the page from the book, and she got less freaked out, and she smoked, and then cussed for no reason, and she felt better, and then she felt good, so good.

She climbed back in the window, closed it but didn't latch it, and she dropped her jacket to floor, and went downstairs and saw the front door was closed but not locked but she didn't care right now and she sat down on the sofa and watched the news in a haze until she fell asleep.

Chapter Twenty-nine

Seeing Momma Everywhere

This is the next morning, now, and this is how it is:

Thyme wakes up and feels hung over, even though he's had nothing to drink.

He smells his hands and they smell like cigarettes, even though he's had nothing to smoke.

It's not quite light outside, but not still all dark.

His head hurts. The television is on a commercial and he closes his eyes and drifts back into sleep, dreaming of liquor, pot, and cigarettes.

He wakes again and his hands still smell and his head still hurts, and the television is still on. He has to squint; what was mostly dark with a little light awhile ago is now almost all light. There's a woman's voice on the television; he smells his hands again and can taste a cigarette. The voice is familiar. His eyes hurt as he looks from the orange hue in the windows to the television screen in front of him.

He blinks a few times.

A few more times.

No. He can't be awake.

He stands up and gets up off the sofa and walks around the room a few times, swinging his arms back and forth and then he sits down again.

Suzanne.

Momma.

Momma Exler is on the television screen, reading the news to Thyme. He stares at it and then a commercial comes on. He goes over and turns off the television.

He's fallen asleep in his shoes; he can smell them.

He picks his sweatshirt up off the floor, puts it on, strokes his beard, finds his hat and his camera, and walks out the front door into the brisk morning air.

He goes the opposite direction today than he did yesterday.

He's fiddling with his camera, watching his breath in the cold air, still feeling oddly hung over.

There's no side walk here so he's on the street; he doesn't know what day it is, but it must be a weekday he figures by all the people leaving their front doors and walking into the cold morning air to their cars, all with a certain air of boredom and a little resentment around them.

Ah, Thyme thinks to himself, employment.

He doesn't miss it.

He takes a picture of a man across the street that just spilled coffee on his pants, cussing, dropping and kicking his briefcase.

Thyme takes a picture two doors down of two men leaving a house, holding hands, walking to a car parked outside.

Another picture of a man: still in his pajamas, at his front door, groping his wife, who was dressed to go to work.

Thyme takes a picture of a mother closing her skirt in her front door as her two children, both girls, fight on the front steps. Then the woman turns around, and looks right at Thyme as he still has his eye to the view finder of his camera, and the woman looks just like a younger Momma, a younger Suzanne, just like he remembers her to be twenty years ago or so.

A pack of joggers is coming up behind him, seven, maybe eight people, all men, except for two, the one in the front and the one in the back; the one in the back turns and looks at Thyme as she jogs past him; she looks just like Momma.

He stops.

He rubs his eyes. He turns and heads back home.

In a red two-door sedan, parked on the side of the street, he swears, sits Momma, not looking in his direction and blowing on a cup of tea.

He starts to run home, and when he gets home he slams the front door, takes off his hat, and lays the camera on the table.

He turns the channel and a coffee commercial is on with a woman who looks like Suzanne taking a sip of coffee and smiling. But Momma never drank coffee, he thought; she never drank coffee when she was alive, but he's seeing her do it now, and smiling.

Thyme walks to the closest where his tools are.

He finds his hammer.

He walks back to the television and smashes the screen.

This is now, and this is how it is:

At the same time, just a couple miles away, Stan is waking up to the same coffee commercial on the same channel, only he doesn't see Suzanne on the screen.

He can feel his pulse in his swollen, blood crusted nose.

He reaches to the table in front of him and opens the pill container and takes out three pills and swallows them whole without any water and then he switches on some cartoons, and closes his eyes although he remains awake, and he lays there until he can feel the pills begin to take hold, and then he remains there even longer, and he begins to feel so good that even his nose has stopped bleeding.

This is the same time, and this is how it is:

Chastity wakes up, just in her shirt, and she walks over the window and stares out, watching the cars go by, people hurriedly getting their kids to school so they can get to their jobs, their boring jobs, and Chastity is happy she doesn't have to be bothered with that.

Chapter Thirty

Hyposomniac Dreams

This is the next morning, and this is how it is:

Chastity woke up early, on the sofa, and had been dreaming about her mother.

Her mother.

She doesn't even know who her mother is, but she just had a dream and in that dream she knew her, she saw her, she smelled her.

She feels bad.

She wakes up and it's dark outside and she has a faint smell of perfume on her hands, but she doesn't have any perfume.

She wakes up, and she sees a car's red tail lights down the street, and she hears a dog in the distance barking, and the news is on, but it's all news about European markets or the Tokyo markets because it's the East Coast and it's not even seven in the morning and there's nothing going on here yet; the volume on the television is off, she turns it up, and she grabs some socks from the floor and puts them on, and takes the blanket that was covering her during the night from the floor and wraps it around her shoulders. She goes to the kitchen, her kitchen; she starts to makes coffee. She sees a joint on the kitchen counter, she rolled three last night and smoked one, and lost one, and here's the third one; she lights it and smokes it as the coffee maker starts that coughing sound and then the pot smell and the coffee smell join together and for a moment, and she feels she could spend the rest of her life here in this kitchen, her kitchen.

Then she remembers her mother.

A few deep hits on the joint, hold it in, and puff some more before she exhales, and she forgets she's making coffee: that's just how joints work.

She thinks about the woman in the dream, no, the girl in her dream: she's really no more than a child, almost half the age that Chastity is now; maybe sixteen; she's got a boyfriend, older, maybe eighteen. Chastity dreamed about a fight, about the man, the boy really; she dreams about the woman, the girl really, swollen in the belly, pregnant.

She's sixteen and pregnant; he's eighteen and still a child.

There's anger; there's denial; there's fear; there's little hope.

She sees this girl, this young pregnant woman, three decades ago, lost in tears, an embryo kicking her in the stomach, pressing against her bladder, and it's her, it's Chastity.

She smells the coffee and puffs on the joint again and she goes back into the dream.

She hears a shout; she feels a fight in her dream, an argument, confusion. A fight. She realizes that her mother never sees the man again, and that he never knows what she does. He never knew if she had the baby; maybe a miscarriage, an abortion.

Back out of the dream now, the coffee is done, the joint is almost done, and she smokes it until it is too small to smoke, and snuffs it out on the countertop and then eats it. She walks over and opens a cabinet for a mug, then momentarily forgets what she is looking for (that's just how joints word), then she remembers, grabs a mug, pours her coffee into the mug and stares at it until it gets cold.

She sticks the coffee in the microwave and presses one minute and twenty six seconds and stares at the mug in the microwave on the carousel going round and round and when she takes it out, it's hot, steam is rising, and she accidently stumbles a little, shakes just a bit, and drops her coffee mug upside down over her feet. When the black liquid hits, it burns, it burns so much, and she falls on the kitchen floor and cries, but not only because of the burns on her feet.

This is a week later, two weeks even, now, and this is how it is:

Thyme is contacted by his mother's estate attorney.

He goes to see him, wearing the same shoes he's been wearing for more than two weeks. He can smell the shoes when he's on the sofa; he can smell the shoes outside. He hates going to a lawyer's office, but realizes the lawyer may hate having him there just as much: Thyme's unshaven, unshowered, unattached; the stink shows. He looks like an addict.

And that's what he is: an addict who is no longer on drugs, or on anything.

It's been less than a month but that's an eternity for him: no pot, no alcohol, no nothing, no painkillers at all, just a beard, photography, unemployment, and being a bearded skinny skeleton.

The meeting with the lawyer is slow but fast: Thyme is now the owner of the house, Thyme has inherited, after the death taxes and the lawyer's fees, what amasses to Thyme as a small fortune: he won't have to find a job anytime soon . . . not that he was planning to.

Thyme walks home; he hasn't seen his mother driving a car or behind a news desk recently.

He has heard those dog tags though, the ones he hears, but never sees. He wonders why he sees his dead Momma, but not his dog. He wonders why he sees her, Momma, alive, with ghostly dogs he doesn't recognize, but he hears his dog, the one he and Maria loved so much, he can smell it even, but he can't see it, and he can't see her, Maria, although he's trying to remember what color eyes she has, had, or the dog, too, what color eyes did the dog have?

He gets home, looks in the mirror, and sees his bearded face and he thinks about Momma, and then drops onto the floor and cries for hours.

Now it's now, a little later, and this is how it is:

Thyme, a bearded skinny skeleton, is out of the bathroom and sitting on the sofa, happily unable to watch the news on the shattered television, thinking about pills he no longer has, thinking about home grown herb he no longer has, and he's sitting there thinking about Momma: Momma dying in her fast car, Momma dying fast in her car, Momma dying face first against the windshield, and he sits there, thinking about Momma (who he no longer has), and does nothing but grow his beard and think about time (which is all he has).

This is a little later that night, now, and this is how it is:

Chastity is asleep on the sofa in her house.

She's dreaming that she's watching television, a cooking show with two women and a man with a studio audience; Chastity's not sure if it's a program or an infomercial; she's getting hungry; she can almost smell the food through the television screen. The woman on the television starts to speak to her, the woman says, "Chastity, honey, do you get it? Did you write it down? Do you need us to go over this again?" And the woman pauses, the whole show appears to pause, and Chastity looks around the room, her empty living room, and the three hosts are staring at the camera, waiting for Chastity to answer, and the crowd in the studio is quiet, the television screen flashes to an announcer with a large headset on, he's waiting for her to say something, and she looks at the television and whispers, "Oh, no, I'm fine, please, go ahead." The two women and the man then start cooking again, the audience is clapping again while the show's announcer waxes poetic about allspice. The man leaves the scene, there was some joke but Chastity wasn't really paying attention anymore, and it's just the two woman on the screen, and they keep on cooking but the one who stopped the show for Chastity just a minute ago is addressing Chastity the whole time she's mixing ingredients and she's saying, "Chastity, not too much salt," and "You're going to love this one, Chastity, you'll eat it all day long." The woman suddenly stops talking and stops cooking and ignores the show, although it continues to go on around her, and suddenly she is Suzanne; Momma is on the television show: Momma is looking through the television at Chastity, looking her right in the eyes, but just for a moment. Just for a moment, and then she goes back to cooking, to mixing, to chopping and she stops addressing Chastity, and then that dream dies and another begins.

In this next dream, she is there in the cemetery, the one that is in all of her dreams; she's not a child in this dream, it's now, and she's in corduroy pants with three pennies in her pocket, and she's walking through the cemetery. She doesn't hear her foster father's voice, and she doesn't see Stan lurking behind a headstone, but she does see a stone that says Exler on it. She walks closer and sees that there are now two headstones, one for Suzanne, and one for Thyme, which has no date of death on it, and Chastity reaches into her pocket, and she takes out one of the pennies, and she puts it on top of Suzanne's headstone. She's standing there in the cold wind, when all of a sudden, she hears her foster father's voice calling her, she becomes half her size suddenly and twenty-five years younger and she's holding a penny in each hand, her last two, as she runs away from the Exler headstones with the penny on top.

She runs, as a child, to her foster father, who's holding the drawing she made of them, and he's smiling, and she's smiling, and she hugs him, and her dream goes hazy, and she just sleeps after that without any more dreams.

Thyme is awake at odd hours. With no drugs, no uppers, no downers, no smokes, sometimes his brain and his body are on different wavelengths.

He sometimes thinks he's awake all night, only to be dreaming that he's awake; he'll think he's up all night and then he'll suddenly wake up, sweaty, from a dream that became a nightmare.

He stares at the television, the smashed one, and he tries to will it to work, but it just sits there, smashed. And he sits there, envious of the screen for being smashed.

He's on the sofa, doing nothing but wasting time. It's dark outside, and he closes his eyes, just for a second, a minute, then two, and then he's dreaming.

He's dreaming that he's back in the graveyard, the cemetery that Momma is buried in, and he's walking around, disoriented, and he wanders and wanders seemingly for hours, but the sun never seems to change over head and the clouds don't move. Then he's there, looking down at Momma's grave, at her headstone, and there's a penny on top of it, and he looks at it and then he picks it up and puts it in his pocket, and then he hears laughter, a child's laughter, and across the cemetery he can see a young girl hugging a man, maybe her father. They are looking at a piece of paper that they are holding between them.

And then Thyme wakes up.

He's back on the sofa, his hands in his pocket, his beard growing, and the television still busted. He wakes, and when he scratches his nose, his fingers smell like pennies.

It's 6 a.m.

It's time to take a walk.

This is fifteen minutes later, Thyme's gotten up off the sofa, and found some warm clothes: a scarf, his hat, the same pair of pants, and his sockless tennis shoes, and he walks out the front door with his camera bouncing around his neck, and starts walking to the cemetery.

He's walking faster than normal; it's cold.

Within fifteen or twenty minutes, he's walking around the headstones, the camera bumping against his chest as keeps his hands in his pocket for warmth. He's almost there. It's getting light. Thyme still sees the moon in the distance, as if slacking around to see the sun rise. He stands in front of Suzanne's grave for a minute, silently. He doesn't cry.

He takes a picture of her grave, of the headstone, and of the outline of new dirt.

Then he reaches into his pocket; he takes out a penny. He smells it.

He puts it on top of his mother's headstone, and then, closer than before, he takes a picture of the penny resting on top of the headstone. He realizes he is stepping on his mother's grave, so he quickly backs up three steps and starts walking away, back towards the road.

As he's walking away from Momma's grave, he sees a woman, also dressed for the cold, walking in his direction. He lifts up his camera and takes her picture.

She stops for a second, then continues walking, walking right towards Thyme.

He can see her breathe in the air.

She walks closer, without making any eye contact and without saying anything, and then she's right in front him.

She doesn't say anything to him, and he doesn't say anything to her.

She smiles, and looks down at her hand, then opens her palm between them, and Thyme sees a penny in her hand. She walks around him, goes up to Momma's headstone, and places her penny on top of the one that Thyme had put there just minutes ago.

She turns and walks past him, still silent, and she walks back out the way she came in; Thyme is following slowly behind her, he has to go that way anyway; he doesn't walk too slowly and she never speeds up.

Thyme is following Chastity, thinking about photography, unemployment, and the smell of cold pennies.

It's a couple of hours later, now, and this is how it is:

The sun is up; it's a little warmer outside and the streets are full of morning commuters.

With his nostril bleeding, Stan Thimble doesn't care about people going to their jobs, he doesn't care that he doesn't have a job, and he doesn't care to start looking for one.

He's doing nothing. Nothing.

Well, not right now.

He's not doing Nothing right now: This is right now, and this is how it is:

Stan and his bleeding nostril are in his car, and he just gave the finger to a teenager who cut him off in traffic, and he's listening to loud rock, but he can't sing along because it makes his nose bleed more. He's driving to Chastity's house. He remembers the address from the hospital forms.

He's doing nothing right now but driving, to her house; when he gets there, he has no plan. Maybe he'll just drive on by.

But he doesn't.

Stan pulls into the driveway. He pulls in behind the blue car in the driveway; he leaves the engine on.

He sees lights on in the first floor windows; the front door is shut; the upstairs rooms are all dark, the bedrooms, her bedroom (he smiles as he thinks of this room), they're all dark. He sees that one of the bedroom windows is open a little; the curtains hang and dance, lazily, in the winter breeze.

The car is still running, wasting gas; he unfastens his seat belt and opens the door, and gets out of the car, slowly. He walks to his left, away from the front door, and he walks beside the garage, then around the back of the house, and takes another right turn and he's walking back to the front of the house. He hesitates at the front door. He ambles slowly through the grass, and sits in his car, closes the door, turns up the radio, listens for a minute or two, backs out of the driveway, and fastens his seat belt as he's stopped in the middle of the street; then he puts the car in gear and drives off.

Chastity, a little stoned, sat upstairs in the library of her house, slowing smoking a joint as she sat on the floor and stared out the partially opened window at Stan sitting in his car in her drive way. She saw him get out and walk around the side of her house and disappear, and she didn't even flinch, that must be the weed, because she didn't even start to sweat when he walked by the front door, which she knew was unlocked.

Then she saw him get into his car, taking his time, backing out into the street, pausing there for a minute, and then she watched him put on his seatbelt and drive off.

This was a couple of hours before that, then, and here's how it was:

Thyme and Chastity had previously only spoken that handful of words, around here, in the cemetery, after Suzanne's burial.

Thyme walked towards his house, which from the cemetery is the same direction as Chastity's for a while. He walked behind her, not too far, not too close, for ten minutes. Then came the time for her to turn, so she did, and she looked back over her shoulder and turned a little, and Thyme, then catching up to the cross road, held up his hand where she'd shot him, and he said towards her through his beard: "Wasn't the first time that I'd been shot."

She doesn't say anything.

So he smiles.

He strokes his beard.

He stops in the middle of an intersection; no cars are coming; he pulls the neck of his sweatshirt, he can hear some tearing in the seams, he stops pulling the neck and pulls his arm out of the sleeve and then lifts up the sweatshirt and his t-shirt underneath it and shows his shoulder, he nods to his shoulder and the scar, "I've been shot worse. It's okay."

He continues to smile. She begins to smile.

Then she turns and walks on, and he sticks his arm back into its sleeve and turns and walks home to his smashed television set.

But, before he does walk off, he snaps a couple frames of her, walking away from him.

This is later that day, that night, and this is how it is:

Thyme is asleep, on the sofa, and he is dreaming that his television is working: he is dreaming that the stock market is doing well, he's dreaming that he won't have high heating bills this winter, he's dreaming that there was no violence in the Middle East today, he's dreaming that the fighting in Africa had stopped, he's dreaming that he has a pocket full of painkillers, he's dreaming he's seeing his mother as a chef on an infomercial on the television, the same television that was smashed when he laid down on the sofa, just a little while ago.

Chastity is not asleep on the sofa; she's gone to the hardware store and bought new locks for the doors, locks for the windows, a hatchet, an axe, and then, from a toy store, a solid wood baseball bat (she tried to find a way to steal one, but couldn't; she's a virgin, not an angel).

Now it's now, in the early morning darkness, and this is how it is:

Everyone's asleep.

Everyone's dreaming of Momma Exler on their television screens.

Everyone's smiling.

Chapter Thirty-one

Insomniac Visions

Now it's now, the next day, and this is how it is:

Stan, whose left nostril is not bleeding right now (just wait), is at the mall getting a new cell phone. He wants one with a good camera.

He finds one, buys it, and now he has a new phone, with a better camera.

He walks back to his car and sits behind the wheel, with the engine running, and looks at his new phone and tests the camera on a young mother who walks by pushing a stroller into the mall.

Click.

View.

Smile.

It's been a while since he's had sex; it was with Erin, the last time; he wishes he still had that phone; he looks down at the burn on his hand, and his left nostril begins to bleed; no matter what she did, Stan liked her. He'd like to see her again, all of her again.

He sees another woman walking towards the entrance: Click, view, smile, repeat.

This is later, now, and this is how it is:

Chastity has left an axe next to the front door, the hatchet near the back door in the kitchen, and the baseball bat next to the sofa she sleeps on; she's installed the locks on the windows, she's changed the old locks on the door and installed a deadbolt on the back door, where there wasn't one before.

She closed and locked the windows on the first floor; she closed the blinds in all the windows, and then switched on the television and went numb watching the news talk about unemployment.

She switches the channel with the remote.

She's resting her foot on the baseball bat that's rolling on the floor near the sofa; she's still under dressed for the season, though she does have socks on. She likes the feel of the baseball bat under her socked foot; she likes the idea of swinging it if she has to, or wants to.

She falls asleep for a little while.

She's dreaming about running around as a child in socked feet, and dragging a plastic yellow baseball bat behind her. In her dream, she bends down to pick some clovers, there are a dozen four leaf clovers right at her feet. She drops the plastic baseball bat, which is now pink in her dream, and she drops to her knees and starts picking clovers, one, then two, and then another. Then she hears the sound that ends of all her dreams these days, the sound of a foster father calling her. She leaves the baseball bat there and runs to show her foster father the clovers that she's found, and she runs to the front yard where he is, and she runs up to him. When she gets there, she opens her hands but she no longer has clovers, there are now two pennies in one hand and one in the other.

She wakes up; her foot is still resting on the baseball bat.

She looks into her left hand, she's holding two pennies.

She opens her right hand, and there's nothing in it.

This is the next morning, 7 a.m., and this is how it is:

Thyme's awake, and in the kitchen.

He's been up since 5:15 a.m.

He is in the kitchen, leaning against the counter, doing nothing.

He snaps out of his blankness, and decides to make himself a cup of tea.

He has the radio on; it's tuned to NPR. Nothing special in the weather, it's cold and there are no flowers alive, but there is a special report about lice in the school system around him. He stands there, watching his tea steep, and his head begins to itch.

He scratches as he listens to the news story on the radio. The more the two correspondents (who Thyme hears daily every morning as he's alone in the kitchen) talk about the lice in the elementary school the more his head itches, then his sideburns, then his whole beard.

It's now 7:15 a.m.

He opens the drawer to the left of the sink that holds the large knives and brings out a big black pair of scissors. He listens to the voices on the radio, with one hand he holds meat scissors, and his other hand is constantly scratching his hair.

Down the hall, in the half bath, he turns on the light and stares at himself in the mirror. He likes his beard. He wishes he could have a longer one; he can't believe he spent so many years without one. He stares at his eyes; there's no red, at least not much.

He turns on the two facets in the sink and waits for the water to warm up, scratching his head and listening to the voices in the other room.

But now it's onto another story on the radio.

He stops listening.

He puts his finger into the water; it's warm. He holds his hands in a cup under the water, bends over fully dressed, and douses his hair with water. He doesn't have long hair, but it is shaggy. He begins to run his left hand through his hair and grab some of the longer bangs, the longer side that hangs down over his ear, and he beings to snip and cut away, first on his right side, and then on his left side, and then on the top, and then in the back, all with just the mirror on the wall in the bathroom. Hair falls down into the sink; after a while he scoops up some and tries to get it into the trash and then he washes the other strands down the drain. He keeps cutting and cutting and snipping and snipping and he misses some here and cuts some a little too short there, but he basically gets it.

The radio is on to a sports segment.

He couldn't care less.

Thyme goes upstairs and in the other bathroom he turns on the shower and takes off his sweatshirt and then one t-shirt and then the other.

Then he stares at his shoes.

He stares at his shoes that have been there on his feet ever since Momma lay there dead in her fast car, dead fast in her car, as Momma lay dying; instead of taking them off and taking a full shower he bends his naked torso into the shower stall and shampoo's his newly cut hair and then rinses it and the whole time water is running down his back and getting his pants and the floor wet.

He turns off the shower and dries off and gets dressed and doesn't look into the mirror again.

Now it's now, just a little later, and this is how it is:

Thyme and his newly cut hair are sitting on the front stoop, in the cold, with shoes on but no socks, and he's dying for a cigarette.

He hears the trash truck coming up the street; it's driving for a minute and then Thyme hears a door slam, and then it's driving again, and then a slam. Thyme's still sitting on the stoop, watching absently as the truck gets closer. He can see the writing on the side: Conroy & Son, Refuse Service.

He scratches his newly cut hair; he thinks about lice. He keeps scratching.

The truck pulls up in front of his house and Thyme realizes that he hasn't pulled his trash bin from the side yard, so he gets up and drags his big barrel around to the back of the truck.

Thyme is a little out of breath; he looks at the son from Conroy & Son, and says, "This is a two man job for sure."

The trash man looks at Thyme; says, "Yeah, that's the truth."

"You need someone just to drive this thing; you can't be doing this by yourself."

There's a pause; then the son continues, "Then you drive it for me."

"I'm not looking for a job."

"I didn't offer to pay you."

"Where's your dad?"

The trash man shakes his head 'no' and then says, "Sorry to read about your mother, too."

They shake hands.

"I'm Lincoln. Linc."

"Thyme."

"Get in the driver's side."

"Okay."

Thyme walks around to the driver's side door and opens it, and gets behinds the idling engine, adjusts the left exterior mirror, and slowly pulls the truck down the street as Lincoln holds onto the back, shouting "Take a left here and slow down at the third house; then three more houses down; then the next right."

Thyme turns off the radio in the cab, so much as to hear Lincoln better as to just have nothing to listen to except the moaning of the truck's engine and Linc shouting out directions.

He stopped after three houses. He could feel the truck shift, just a little, as Linc jumped off, and a then a little more, but just a little, when Linc jumped back on.

Then he drove past three more houses and slowed to a stop again; when Lincoln slapped the left side of the truck, Thyme drove off and took the next right, and then he stopped at the third house.

He keeps on driving for a while, a half an hour, maybe forty minutes; he takes a left, and at the third house in he stops, and looks to his side as Lincoln jumped off the truck, and he saw he was right there in front of her house, in front of Chastity's house.

Thyme looks at the front door of the house, Chastity's house, and it's shut. He looks at the ground level windows to the left of the door, and the ones to the right; they're all shut: blinds have been shut in all the windows on the ground floor.

He looks up to the next floor.

The same for two of them, he sees; two are shut off from the outside world tight; but the last window has the blinds up, and some fresh air is going in thru a small gap.

The truck idles.

Thyme gazes up at the window and then he sees her, Chastity. She's been sitting there in the lower part of the window this whole time, looking out at Thyme, as he sat there staring at the other windows. He looks up at her, they exchange glances for a second, and then Lincoln slaps on the back of the truck and Thyme eases his foot off the brake and pulls the truck up another three houses, and then stops, and as Lincoln jumps off the back of the truck, Thyme watches through the side mirror back at Chastity's house, but sees nothing, and then Lincoln slaps the side of the truck and it's time for Thyme to go up to the next corner and hang a right.

Lincoln tells Thyme: "When it gets dark, it's quitting time."

"Whatever," Thyme says through his beard, "I don't have any plans." He smiles.

Lincoln slaps the back of the truck and they start rolling down the street.

It's dark and so it's quitting time and both Thyme and Lincoln are in the cab of the truck; Thyme remains in the driver's seat.

"So, what, are you in a hurry?" Linc asks Thyme, "I'll buy you some beers for helping."

"Okay."

Lincoln directs Thyme to a bar he knows. It takes Thyme ten minutes to find a place to park the truck, and then another ten to actually park it; Lincoln laughs the whole time.

They find a table in the bar; Lincoln pulls out a pack of cigarettes and throws them on the table between them and then pulls a lighter from his pocket and places it on the table next to his right hand.

He looks at the table next to theirs, it's empty and it has an ashtray and the one they're sitting at doesn't have one; Lincoln stands up and reaches over and grabs the ashtray and puts it between Thyme and himself on the table. It's empty.

Thyme is biting his lips; his fingers can feel a cigarette in them. He can taste it.

Lincoln absently picks up the lighter and taps the bottom on the table.

His right knuckles have L I N C tattooed on them.

A waitress comes over, a white college-aged girl who recognizes Lincoln and looks at Thyme, smiles pleasantly, and then looks back to Lincoln, asking, "What can I get for you tonight?"

"Two of my regulars."

She smiles and they smile back at her.

Lincoln is still holding the lighter in his hands; Thyme has been eyeing the pack of cigarettes in the middle of the table this whole time. The pack is already opened and looks a little more than half-full.

Lincoln looks over at Thyme and smiles and says, "What, today was the first day you've driven a trash truck, huh? Not bad."

"Well, I don't really drive much, not in a while actually."

"You get popped?"

"What?"

"Popped, for drunk driving or something?"

"Oh, no, not that, not anything really; I just don't have a car, and don't want to pay the insurance, and I like to walk anyway.

"Yeah, I see you walking sometimes. Anyway, thanks for the help today."

Thyme nods. He glances around the room to see if he recognizes anyone; he doesn't, but it's still early and he'll watch the door all night. It's not a big city, and it's easy to run into people, even though he never wants to.

Lincoln drops the lighter onto the table and looks at Thyme and asks, "So, what happened to your mother?"

Thyme hesitates, then replies, "I think she always wanted to be a racecar driver; she just missed one turn and hit a tree."

"Man," Lincoln says slowly, turning his head from left to right, and he reaches out and grabs the pack of cigarettes from the middle of the table and holds them in his right hand.

"What happened to your pop?"

"Yeah," he says and then promptly drops the pack of cigarettes onto the table, "That was a heart attack. From out of the blue, too. Kind of."

"Kind of?"

"Well, you know," and with that Lincoln points at the opened pack of smokes between them, "forty years or what not."

The waitress comes up to the table, sets a beer in front on Lincoln and then one in front of Thyme, as she leaves, she smiles at Lincoln and winks.

When she's out of range, Thyme smiles and says, "She knows who's paying tonight, huh?"

"Yeah, cheers, boy." Lincoln lifts up his glass and Thyme does the same and they clink glasses in the air, over the ash tray, and both take long sips. "Ahhh."

"Tastes good," Thyme says, "It's been a while since I had a beer."

"Yeah, I don't hear so many bottles in your trash."

Thyme looks at Lincoln; he doesn't know how to respond, so he doesn't say anything.

Linc laughs and continues: "Hey, you do this as long as I do, you notice things. Just like a mailman; the mail man can always figure what's going on. He'll feel the heavy credit card statements; he'll see the magazines in paper wrappers; he'll see someone sending out a lot of cards and not getting any back."

"You like doing this? Doing that? The trash?"

"The refuse, you mean," Lincoln says, laughing.

"Yeah, the refuse," Thyme smiles, and takes another sip of beer.

"Yeah, I do. I like being outside, not having to work in some damn kitchen or office. I've always liked going to the dump. I'd do dumpster diving; you know: get things out that aren't too bad off and fix them up. I like working for myself. I like not having to deal with too many people; they pay their bills because they think the trash is handled by the mafia; customers don't seem to interact too much with me; most people aren't home when I come by: they're at work."

"Work must suck," Thyme smiles.

"But I use it to my advantage with the ladies; the women love it." Lincoln says this with confidence but Thyme lifts an eyebrow and cocks his head. "Sure, man, sure. After I shower of course, and then I get dressed up in some retro clothes, and I go out to a bar, and I buy a woman and drink and take it over and give it to her and they'll say 'Who are you?,' and every time I respond, 'Baby, I'm the trash man; I'm the trash man, baby.' Just like that; the same way every time."

Lincoln stops talking and takes a deep drink from his glass.

"Are you messing with me? Does that really work?"

Lincoln puts down the beer and smiles and looks Thyme in the eyes and says, "Almost every time, my brother, almost every single time."

Cheers again.

"But I'll got to tell you, man," Linc stops talking, smiles to himself, and takes a sip.

"What's that?"

"It works a lot more since there's been a black man in the White House."

"Right on, Linc."

Cheers again, with long, deep drinks into the glasses and they finish their beers. Linc waves the waitress over for another round.

Thyme finally asks Lincoln: "Hey, are you going to smoke one of those things?"

Lincoln smiles and looks at the pack and picks up his beer and then slowly sips it, and then puts it down and says, "No."

Thyme waits a second, a minute, sips his drink, and then, confused, asks, "Why not?"

"It's not my pack."

Thyme raises his eyebrow.

Lincoln continues, "That's my dad's pack of smokes. It was his last pack. I'll never smoke one again. I just carry them around to remind me not to smoke."

Thyme tells Lincoln he'll walk home and thanks for the beers and Lincoln again thanks Thyme for the help. Thyme says he'll help him again tomorrow; Lincoln says, "I can't pay you right now."

"Then don't pay me; I'm not looking for a job anyhow."

"I'll pick you up in the truck in the morning."

Thyme gets up and leaves and then he sees Lincoln talking with the waitress and he can hear him say to her, "Baby, I'm the trash man; I'm the trash man, baby." And he sees the waitress smile and then sit in the chair that Thyme just vacated, and she reaches over and touches Lincoln's hand, and Thyme closes the door behind him and takes a left onto the sidewalk, and begins to walk home.

He takes a detour; he walks past Chastity's house. He tells himself a lie; he tells himself that he's just looking for trashcans for his route this day next week; tomorrow will be a new route.

He stops in front of Chastity's house; all of the windows are dark. The car is in the driveway, and the blinds are down in the window that Thyme saw Chastity looking out of this morning. Thyme stands there for a minute and then walks on home; he wishes he had his camera with him, he wishes he had a cigarette.

This is the next morning, now, and this is how it is:

It's about 7:30 a.m., Thyme is sitting on his front steps watching cars go by; it's cold and he can see his breath in the air. It reminds him of smoking. He's thinking about that nicotine rush; he's thinking about that taste of the first cigarette of the day.

He turns around and goes inside, grabs his baseball hat and some work gloves, and his camera, letting it dangle from his neck.

He looks over at the busted television set out of habit.

He had mentioned to Lincoln the night before that he loved photography and, between beers, Lincoln told him he'd like to see some of his photos. Thyme walked down the hall to his room and grabbed two of his mid-sized portfolio books, and went back to the front porch.

As he locks the front door, he hears Lincoln's truck coming down the street. Thyme checks the door, pockets his keys, and walks to the truck, with the two portfolios under his arm.

Lincoln is getting out of the truck as Thyme arrives at the driver's side.

"You might as well drive."

"Doesn't matter to me."

Lincoln went around to the passenger side and got in and slammed the door; Thyme put his portfolio and camera behind the seat and started the truck's engine. Neither one is wearing their seat belts.

Just as Thyme is about to pull out, he sees a red car he's seen a handful of times; Stan Thimble's red car, and he can see Stan in the driver's seat, with a bandaged nose, looking through the window towards Thyme's house. Stan doesn't see Thyme.

"Son of a . . . !" Thyme shouts, and grabs the wheel tighter.

Lincoln looks at Thyme, then out the front window, and then back at Thyme again. "What?"

"Nothing, nothing; let's get on with it. Which way?"

Then they pull out from Thyme's house, going the opposite direction than Stan. Thyme is happy to be getting farther away from him.

Now it's later, two p.m., and this is how it is:

Thyme has been listening to the radio, scratching his head again after hearing another report on lice in area schools while going three houses and stopping for a couple of minutes until he hears Lincoln slap the side of the truck, then he pulls down three or four more houses and lets Lincoln run down a driveway and grab a big plastic trashcan and wheel it down the to the truck, empty it, and then leave it there at the curb, and then slap!

Thyme moves on.

Time moves on.

Now he's stopped, waiting on Lincoln; he can hear the wheels of a trash can coming down the driveway.

A couple of joggers jog past the truck, as it idles in the street.

He is gazing out the window, listening to cellos on the radio, waiting patiently for the next talk radio program to come on, and then he sees her walking down the street. This is a new street to Thyme, he's never been on it before and it's not near her house. She's almost right next to the big truck, right next to the driver's side window.

And then she's there, here, right next to the window, right next to Thyme.

And she stops.

And she turns her head, and looks up to the window.

And her face, which had been expressionless, turns into a smile, and she raises one hand and waves; in the other hand she is holding a plastic shopping bag. He recognizes the bag; it's one of the ones from the store he used to work at. She turns walks in front of the truck to the passenger side; she reaches up and opens the door; Thyme can hear Lincoln rolling a bin closer.

Thyme looks over.

"I'm Chastity." She climbs into the cab of the truck and sets her shopping bag between her feet on the floor. "I don't think I've actually introduced myself before."

Slap!

Thyme looks into the mirror and pulls forward; "No. I don't think you did." He drives four houses forward this time, and then stops, his foot pressing on the brake. He looks over, scratches his head, smiles, and says, "I'm Thyme."

He extends his right hand; they shake hands.

Slap!

He eases his foot off the brake and the truck eases forward.

Thyme moves on.

Time moves on.

Chapter Thirty-two

Arson, Homelessness

Thyme continues to drive the truck.

Chastity says she didn't know he was the trash man; Thyme smiles, says he's not the trash man, but points towards Lincoln and says, "He's the trash man."

After a minute, he continues, "This isn't even my job; I'm just helping him out. I don't really have much to do."

Chastity smiles back at him, "Me either."

It's quiet for a few minutes, and Chastity says to Thyme, "You know, I've read one of your mom's books."

"I haven't, actually."

"Is *Time's Passing* about you?"

Slap!

"I never asked that; I never asked her too much about her stuff; she was very personal about it."

"I read *Time's Passing*, almost just in passing, I just happened to come across a copy of it. Later I rolled a joint with a page from it."

Thyme smiles, and says, "That sounds like a reasonable idea. Momma would have smiled if she had heard that."

Chastity begins to say something and then she stops talking before she even started again, and she looks out the front window, at nothing, and then there's a knock on the passenger window, and she rolls it down, and Lincoln is standing there, and he smiles up at her in the cab and he says, "Baby, I'm the trash man. I'm the trash man, baby." Then Lincoln smiles and he wheels a can to the back of the truck.

"That's his pick-up line," Thyme says to Chastity, "It got him laid last night I believe."

She smiles and says, "That won't get him laid with me." She's thinking: I'm a virgin, not an angel.

Slap!

Thyme pulls forwards a few houses and then slows to a stop again.

"Is that your new camera?" Chastity is looking behind the seat.

"New?" Thyme listens for Lincoln's wheels coming to the truck, "Yeah. That's my new one, alright."

"I have your old one."

Slap!

"Sorry? What?" Thyme looks over towards Chastity. "What did you say?"

"I have your old camera. It's broken anyway. I'm sorry. I'm a virgin, not an angel."

Thyme just looks at her, confused.

"And I saw your mother on television the other day, on a cable cooking show."

Thyme nods his head, "I've been seeing Momma everywhere." He scratches his head again; the voices on the radio make him think of the lice; he's not so sure he doesn't have them now.

They sit as the engine idles and Thyme can hear the wheel of a trash bin nearby, and then a lighter sounding roll, and then: Slap! He turns a corner, to the left this time, and stops at the third house on the block.

She stares down the road, to the right, while Thyme stares to the left. She says, "I used to live in a house on this block. In that house down there, the fifth one. I lived there from when I was eleven until I was thirteen."

"Yeah?"

"A foster home."

"Ah. I see."

"Gawd, I haven't thought about that place in forever."

She just stares at it.

Slap! The truck rolls forward a few houses.

"That was the second house I used to be fostered in that we passed today, since you picked me up."

"I picked you up?"

"In the truck."

He smiles, says, "Seems to me you just got in the truck; not that it's a problem or anything. Good to have company."

She goes on like she never heard him, and says, "That was the second house, and they look so different than they used to; all fresh, fresh colors, new windows. Why is it that I always remember the places I used to live being a different color? And the same color, too; isn't that weird?"

He's taking a right turn, making sure he doesn't drop Linc in the process, and he asks her, "What color? What color do you remember them as?"

"Drab green. Olive green."

"Oh."

"Seems like a lonely job, this, just driving in the cab all day, stopping and starting and stopping, alone."

"Well, it's not even my job."

He continues, "And I get to listen to the radio all day. I've been burned out on watching television all day."

Slap!

The truck slows to a stop.

Lincoln comes around to the driver's side and says it's time to head home. Thyme scoots into the middle of the seat, with Chastity to the right of him by the window, and Linc taking over the wheel.

Traffic has picked up; it's getting dark, and the after-work traffic has started. Lincoln keeps his gloves on as he drives; he says this time of year, his hands stay cold all day and night. "I almost sleep with these gloves on."

Lincoln finds where Chastity lives, and based on where they were right now, he said he'd drop Thyme off first, and then take Chastity home, "If that's all right with you, baby."

"Driving me home is the closest you'll get to sleeping with me, if that's what you're trying to get at."

Lincoln smiles, scratches his chin with his tattooed right hand, and says, "I already got a date tonight." He smiles over at Chastity, and then to Thyme and says to him, "The same waitress from last night."

"Again?"

"Again. I told you: it works every time."

Chastity responds, "Not every time."

Lincoln half-lies, "I was only half-trying with you."

This is now, about fifteen minutes later, and this is how it is:

Coming down Thyme's street, the traffic is blocked off near his house. Chastity gets out and moves a sign so Linc's truck can get down the street to Thyme's house. The police cars that are on the side of the road do not have their sirens on, but the flashing lights are all on. An ambulance is pulling away in no hurry without any emergency lights on, going down the street away from the approaching trash truck.

And there are two fire trucks and a fire department suburban and two other cars with smaller red lights on top and the fire department insignia on the front door and hood.

Thyme's two story house is now a one story house of broken windows and blackened, peeling siding. The roof appears to have collapsed on the where the second floor once was.

Smoke is rising.

The area is taped off; spotlights are on the house.

Water from hoses is still being sprayed onto the house, but Thyme, Lincoln, and Chastity can see from the front seat of the truck that the fireman are not acting urgently, one is drinking coffee, one is packing up a hose. It looks like more or less a complete loss, Thyme sees, what the fire didn't get, the smoke and water would've ruined.

Thyme reaches behind the seat and finds his camera, and takes pictures of his smoldering home through the window of the truck.

"Let's just get out of here, Linc. There's nothing here, anymore; it was Momma's house anyway."

Lincoln eases the truck on down the street and Thyme takes one more shot of Momma's smoldering house across Lincoln's profile as they pass by.

Part Five

Unemployment Pills, a Trespasser, & Other Daymares

Chapter Thirty-three

A Slap in the Dreams

This is two and a half weeks later, now, and this is how it is:

Thyme has been living in Chastity's house: homeless and sockless, but not penniless.

This is now, and this is how it is: there's a guest bedroom in Chastity's house, but Thyme doesn't feel at ease there; he's been sleeping on the floor in the library on the second floor. He's been using a sleeping bag that he and Lincoln found in a pile near the curb the day after Momma's house burnt. It has been declared a total loss, Momma's burnt house, and is being investigated for arson.

Thyme knew it was arson, no question about it.

He even knew who did it.

He just didn't care.

Thyme's been in the library of Chastity's house sleeping on the floor; she typically sleeps in front of the cable news, or infomercials; there are two unused bedrooms within feet of where Thyme sleeps.

There are a couple of Suzanne Exler's books in the room. Thyme had never read any of his mother's books before, and over the past couple of weeks he read a couple, on the floor, on his sleeping bag; he could hear Chastity's news shows through the floor.

He hasn't watched television since he smashed his own.

This is now, and this is how it is: It's eight o'clock p.m.; it's dark outside, and Thyme is sitting cross-legged on the floor, sockless, with filthy shoes on; he can smell them.

He's combing his beard with his right hand, his good hand. After a while, he'll scratch his hair; he hasn't gotten past that lice scare not too long ago. He has a glass of room temperature tap water on the floor near him.

He's wearing his favorite pants; his sweatshirt, too; his hat is within sight. His sunglasses are on the third shelf from the bottom on the bookshelf, the one that Chastity is sitting in front of, looking towards Thyme.

She's in socked feet.

Clean socks.

She's in a t-shirt, that's too big for her; it looks like the same one Thyme wore two days ago. Her t-shirt is plain white, with white paint spills, white on white; white socks, too.

She's nursing a joint.

She's using a coffee mug as an ashtray; she's smiling.

She hits the joint, and taps off the end into the mug, and then leans back against the book shelf, glances up to make sure nothing is falling down on her, and then stops smiling for a second, then starts smiling again.

"I've decided to wait until spring until I get a job. Until I start looking for a job." He raises his eyebrow, he hasn't spoken in a few minutes, and Chastity continues: "Until I start thinking about looking for a job."

She hits the joint.

He says, "That's more like it." Smiling. Nodding. Smelling the air, the smoke hanging heavily in the room.

She doesn't even bother passing the joint to him; he declined the first three days and she stopped asking after that.

"What day is it? What day is tomorrow?"

"Tuesday," she says.

"Today or tomorrow?"

"Does it matter?"

He pauses; smiles; shakes his head no. "I guess Linc's gonna pick me up in the morning. To work."

She laughs a little, smoke comes out of her nose and she coughs and then says, in a chuckle, "Hmmm, 'work'."

"Oh, it is work, all right; I'm driving all day; driving by the neighborhoods three houses at a time."

"And not getting paid for it."

"That's right," he reaches for his glass of water and lifts it into the air in a cheers, she lifts her joint into the air for her cheers, and then he takes a sip and she takes a hit, and he says, "working, just not getting paid for it."

"I'm thinking of looking for something I can do from home. Like, stuff boxes with medical supplies. Stuff envelopes with coupons. Sell some pills on the side maybe. Or maybe I can design an envelope that has morphine in the glue, people will love to send letters again, they'll be addicted to my envelopes. Or maybe I can sell sex toys, with some of those sex toy parties for housewives. Of course, I won't be able to answer any of the questions about the toys; but I'll just bring you along with me and you can help."

"Why not?"

"Or phone sex maybe."

"Phone sex?"

"Yeah, 1-800-vir-gins."

"Virgin phone sex?"

"I don't see why not." She hits her joint. "With men it's so easy that you, any of you, can just hear me, never mind look at me, and that's that. I could make good money just lying in the bed, lying on the phone. I'm a virgin and I could do it; I'm a virgin and I could make you blue over the phone."

"I don't see why not." He pauses and stares at the bookshelf behind her, he sees his sunglasses and a copy of one of his mother's books, and he goes on, "It is easy isn't it."

"You know what else I think a good idea would be?"

"What?"

"Having Linc pay you for your job."

"I don't have a job." He winks.

"Oh, yeah, because he doesn't pay you."

"I don't want a job."

"Then don't get one."

"Oh, I won't."

They switch places for a change of view; she asked if he wanted to go down and watch television and he answered, "I'd rather listen to you talk."

She's on his sleeping bag; his back is against the bookshelf and his sunglasses are behind him, on the third shelf.

She clears her throat; smiles a little.

"I taped an adoption certificate to my bedroom walls."

"I didn't think you were ever adopted."

"I wasn't. It was a certificate I found somewhere. In a school library, in a copy of a Shakespeare play. I forget which play now; it's been almost two decades.

"I found it, left the book, never did my report, and took the certificate home. A certificate from the same year I was born. A girl's name, too. Not mine. I'm not going to tell you what the name was; it'll make me cry to say it, and I don't want to cry."

"That's okay."

"I hung it on the wall with scotch tape. I remember stealing the tape from the library too. I never was an angel, I guess."

They smile at each other. Thyme rubs his beard.

She goes on, "I took it from one house to the next, wherever I ended up going to. It got torn a bit, then taped up again, then stepped on, and rained on once, and then it disappeared. I just lost it; it ended up in the landfill, no doubt.

"I always took such comfort in it. That piece of paper. It made me feel like someone wanted me. Just a little. Like I had a place. A home. Not a house, like this. This is no home for me; but this is my house. It's still kind of strange to me. Here. This place."

A pause. He coughs. Closes his eyes for a few seconds, rubs his temple.

She says, "But, no, no one ever adopted me. And I'm too old now, huh?"

"Yeah," he smiles, "A little."

"But I'm younger than you."

"Yeah, a little."

She smiles.

Then he coughs a little, and smiles a lot.

"Here."

"What are these?"

"Take them; they'll help you sleep; I heard you walking around all last night."

"Thanks," he says, and tosses the pills in his mouth and washes then down with some water.

"Good night."

"Night."

He dreams that he's in the grocery store, shoeless, working on a night when Erin is manager; he's stocking shelves, but it's earlier than normal, and there are customers walking around.

He's stocking boxes of tea. He's going through all the boxes, looking at the expiration dates; and they are all expired. He drops each to the floor and every time he does it makes the same 'Slap!' sound that Linc makes on the side of the truck. He drops a box lightly on the floor, and Slap!

He's not paying attention to the people shopping around him, until he looks up and sees Momma walking past him, down the aisle, but she doesn't see him, and she walks on past him, and he's about to say something when he tastes that taste in his mouth, the painkiller taste, so he doesn't say anything to Momma as she walks away, but he turns back around to stock some more tea, and then there's Momma right next to, she wasn't there a second ago, and he drops a box of tea, and it lands Slap! on top of her foot, and she looks down at him and before Thyme can apologize Momma drops a gallon of milk that was in her hand, and she slaps Thyme in the face, Slap!, and she walks off, and then Thyme slips in the milk on the floor and when his head his the floor he wakes up, with a headache.

Slap!

Slap!, even in his dreams; even in his dreams, Slap!

In his dreams he is hearing it: hearing Linc's slap.

His hands must be made out of steel, Thyme thought. He sat up, looked around the room from his sleeping bag on the floor, and then lay back down and closed his eyes.

Slap!

Linc.

Thyme was already wearing his clothes, he went to sleep in them, and so he's ready to go.

When Thyme brushes his teeth, the toothpaste tastes like painkillers, like the painkiller taste that was on his tongue in his dream, right before Momma slapped him.

A minute or so later, he's out in cool air, walking to the trash truck, and he opens the passenger side door and says, "You're early."

"I never went home last night," Linc says and smiles and holds up his tattooed fist and continues, "Baby, I'm the trash man! I'm the trash man, baby!"

Thyme smiles and gets in the cab and they leave; his mouth still has a faint taste of the painkiller flavored toothpaste.

A mile down the street, still en route for today's scheduled pickups, Linc pulls the truck to a stop about a car's length from the car in front of them.

"There's that sphincter-licking crack-slime!" spits Thyme.

"What? Where?"

"Ahead of us. In the car."

Linc stares ahead. "No? Really?"

Thyme nods his head and says, "I wish I had a rolling pin about right now."

They smile at each other, Lincoln cusses under his breath.

They sit in silence.

The light seems to be on an extended red.

Thyme's eyebrows perk-up; he says, "Hey, roll the truck right up to him."

Linc says nothing, just eases his boot off the brake; the massive truck slowly creeps forward. The tires make a full rotation. They're right up on the rear of the red car.

By now Stan, in the red car, has noticed the truck rolling closer, and he taps his brake light a few times, and honks his horn, and the only reply is: Slap!, as Linc slaps the outside of the driver's door with his left hand, and he spits, and they're right up on the little car now, they're actually within an inch and Linc stops the truck.

In the red car ahead of them, from the driver's side window: a middle finger pops out of the driver's side window.

Then Linc and Thyme hear something being shouted from inside of the car; Linc says, "No one talks to me like that, and I don't even know what he said."

He eases his foot off the brake and the truck rolls into the rear of the red car and starts to push it a little, eight inches, then a foot, and then two feet into the intersection ahead of them, under the stale red light, Linc pushes the car three feet out; cars coming with the right of way honk their horns and swerve.

Stan Thimble steps out of the car; from the seats in the truck Thyme can see him stomp on the parking brake before he gets out. Stan starts yelling at Linc, and starts spitting and shouting and flicking him off and takes a few steps towards the trash truck and then looks over in the passenger seat and sees Thyme, and he stops, shakes his finger up and down for a minute, starts to say something, and then stops, yells "Motherflyingfairy!" and gets back in his car, pops off the parking brake, and runs the red light right in front of a minivan.

Thyme and Linc sit at the red light, smile, and turn on the radio.

Chapter Thirty-four

Lincoln Parks

This is later that day, a little while ago, and this is how it was:

Thyme and Lincoln switched jobs on the truck about an hour before the route was over; Lincoln slipped on a rock while trying to ignore a dog and twisted his ankle.

Thyme put on some work gloves, and rode on the back of the truck, letting Lincoln drive the rest of the way.

He was exhausted by the second block.

He was dizzy by the last few blocks, holding onto the back of the truck with the cold wind hitting him on his face, his eyes watering, his knees shaking.

And the slap. That powerful slap.

How did Linc hit the side of the truck so hard? Thyme feels as if he's broken a finger. His left shoulder burns; his right one is not feeling much better.

Lincoln parks the truck in front of Chastity's house. Thyme continues to hold onto the back for a moment; then slowly hobbles towards the house, followed by Lincoln, limping on his ankle.

This is a couple of hours later, now, and this is how it is:

Lincoln's truck is still parked out front. It's dark now. The street outside is dark; Chastity's house is the only one around with lights on.

Chastity's baking bacon on a skillet. "It's easier than cleaning the microwave; I just hate all the grease and stuff."

She's exhaling smoke; she passes it to Thyme who takes it and passes it over to Lincoln, who inhales, then exhales, and then does it all over again, twice. He walks towards the popping bacon and passes the joint to Chastity. She takes it as some grease pops and hits her hand and she yelps and accidently drops the joint down into the pan with the frying bacon.

Linc looks down at the joint frying in the bacon and says, "We'll eat it with the bacon after it's all grease-dried," and then he nods his head repeatedly, with pot smoke still creeping from his nostrils.

There's calm for a minute, a quiet. Chastity and Linc are stoned; Thyme is exhausted, hurting, thinking about a pain pill, tasting it on his tongue, already feeling it spread from his stomach out to the rest of him; his thighs feeling hot, his arms feeling cold.

No one is talking.

Bacon is sizzling; Linc is smiling down at the frying joint.

The grease snaps; Chastity giggles a little.

No talking still.

Then, from outside in the dark, a siren is heard, then two. The blinds are all pulled in the front windows, but are flashing from white to blue to white to red to white to red and then blue, a third siren sounds, they sound like they are just out front.

Sirens on the outside; no talking on the inside.

Chastity stops giggling; Linc is still smiling and smelling the bacon; Chastity turns the burner off. Still no talking.

Thyme knows that Chastity and Linc are stoned; he stops stretching out his shoulders and goes to the front room, and looks through the blinds.

Sirens. Flashing red and blue lights. Uniforms.

He glances back towards the kitchen; Linc is leaning against the counter next to the bacon and Chastity is looking towards Thyme.

Thyme says nothing, so she walks up to the front room and stands next to him.

The lights looked as if they were right in front of the house, but they're actually down a house or so, just behind Linc's truck, and there's a fire truck, an ambulance, and three police cars.

Thyme and Chastity look at each other; he says, "Aren't all of those houses empty?"

She says, "I thought so, yeah."

She smells like pot.

Thyme walks to front door, opens it, and smells outside. "Doesn't smell like a fire."

He closes the door and they walk from the living room to the dining room, on the other side of the front door. They watch. Police are walking around the two story house diagonally down the street; the ambulance waits; the fire truck drives off and is replaced by another ambulance. The red and blue police lights are on, but the sirens are off; the ambulances also are silent now.

Thyme smiles when he sees two paramedics smoking cigarettes.

They watch through the windows for a few more minutes; soon, they are joined by Linc, who is eating bacon with one hand and is holding a newly lit joint in the other.

Soon, Linc and Thyme don their jackets and go outside onto the front steps; Chastity stays inside, "You guys go outside; I'm not wearing underwear."

Thyme stands and Linc sits on the bricks with his back next to the door, smoking the joint casually, occasionally handing it to Chastity when she opens the door and sticks her hand out; she'll shut the door and a minute later it'll open again and she'll pass the joint out to Linc and say at the same time she's exhaling "Brrr" and he smiles and takes the joint and she closes the door.

One of the police cars pulls away, and then one of the ambulances leaves, and then a second police car.

Chastity's front door opens and Linc hands the joint back in.

It's quiet again; no talking again; the flashing red lights from the ambulance animate the empty houses all around. The smoking paramedics have gone inside the house.

A little while later, the joint is gone: Chastity is no longer opening the front door; she's not looking out of the windows; she's on the sofa watching the cable news networks.

Then, as Thyme and Linc are watching silently, the front door of the other house opens and the officer walks out, followed by one paramedic in front of a stretcher, with the other paramedic at the other end, carrying a body under a white sheet. They load the body into the back of the ambulance slowly and close the ambulance door and both lean against it and simultaneously produce cigarette packs, one from a pants pocket, the other from a shirt pocket, and then begin to smoke as the policeman says something to them and then goes to his patrol car and types on his laptop.

"Thyme, I thought you said all of those houses were vacant?"

"They are now."

It's a little while later and Thyme, stone sober, has gone up to the library and has fallen asleep on his sleeping bag; he falls asleep dreaming of the days he used to fall asleep at noon, feeling no pain.

Linc, meanwhile, has smoked two more joints with Chastity, downstairs flipping through the cable channels. After Chastity fell asleep on the sofa, Linc went upstairs to the unused bedroom and feel asleep, his boots hanging off the end of the bed.

The next morning brings a breakfast of leftover bacon.

Then, after they get their full, Thyme and Linc walk past the still-sleeping Chastity and make their way out the front door, making sure to deadbolt it as they go out, and walk to the truck.

Linc is still limping a little, so Thyme says, "You drive. I'll haul and slap." Then Thyme climbs into the passenger side and Linc walks around the front and over to his side and shouts, "Freakingfacefolk!"

Thyme climbs down and walks around to the driver's side of the truck and finds Linc cracking his knuckles and muttering to himself under his breath. His truck was parked facing the wrong direction ("Nobody's parking on this street but us, right?"); the tires on the driver's side are completely flat, rims are resting on pavement.

There's a slash on the tire. Linc and Thyme walk to the rear tires; the same: slashed tires.

"Freakingtushtrash!"

It's a couple of hours later, and Chastity is at the grocery store; it's cold and she's stoned so she drove the car today. She needs bacon, cheese, and grits (she wants the kind that cooks in one minute, not five).

She knows where everything in the store is (so does Thyme), so she doesn't grab a hand basket; she's walking around with the round container of grits under her left arm, the cheese in her right hand, and her left hand clutching a package of bacon. She's looking around for Erin, but doesn't see her.

She walks up to a woman working there, an older woman who works part time, and asks, "Do you happen to know where Erin is?"

The older woman stops stocking rice bags, pauses, and says, "No. Do you?"

Chastity shakes her head no. The older woman continues stocking the bags of rice now, looks to her left, and then back to Chastity and says "We haven't heard from Erin in two days. We guess she quit. I hope she's okay. The other manager went by her house and she wasn't there; her car wasn't there either. Her door was locked but she wasn't there. I think she just got tired of this, here, and finally quit; I would if I were her age."

Chastity nods her head and says, "I guess so."

She walks to the checkout aisle and stands in line. She puts her groceries on the floor, picks up a magazine with one hand, and two packs of gum in the other, which she slips in her pocket as she puts the magazine back in place and picks up her groceries again (she's a virgin, not an angel).

She pays with cash that Linc had given her to buy food with, asks for a paper bag, drops her receipt on the floor, and walks out the door, looking back towards the office one more time to see if Erin had popped in; she was planning on asking Erin to give her the food for free since Erin knew Thyme was living at Chastity's now. She walks out the automatic doors, inhales the cold air, and rushes over towards her car.

It's later that night, a handful of hours later, and this is how it is:

"Have you heard from Erin recently?"

He shakes his beard 'no' and says, "Why's that?"

"Well, I went by the store today to have Erin ring me up so I, so you, so we," she smiles and winks towards him, "wouldn't have to spend Linc's money he gave me."

"Give the change back to Linc."

"That's not the point."

"But, no: I haven't seen her."

"They haven't either."

"Maybe Linc and I will drive over to her place tomorrow in the truck, check it out."

"Are you going to be up for dinner later? I'll be watching the news; you can smoke some with me if you want."

"No. Thanks. I need some sleep. We missed some of the route today; we'll have to make it up tomorrow."

Thyme turns and goes off; Chastity picks up the remote control and turns on the television. She starts with the weather channel, then she changes to the home shopping channel; then she flips onto the real estate channel, listing after listing, but she already owns a house and it seems all the houses around her are for sale; then a blank channel, and she keeps it there for a minute, the blue light, the white noise, the occasional hiss.

She lights up a joint and she sits on the sofa, hits the joint a few times, and stares to where the wall meets the ceiling, and it's blue from the television, and she smokes again, and there's a blue haze, and it's not a white noise anymore, it's a hazy-blue hiss.

Up in the library, Thyme stares out the window for a few minutes. He waits until a car passes. He stares out the window, fogging up the window with his breath, he gets too close to the fog on the window and his beard leaves patterns on the glass.

He's waiting for headlights to pass, tail lights; this is just a game: Wait until the first car passes, and then go to bed.

And then headlights pass. Quietly.

He sees, and rubs his eyes, and walks over to the book shelf, and he picks up a sleeping pill and swallows it with no water.

Then he goes to his sleeping bag and lies down on his back, in his clothes, and closes his eyes and falls asleep. Every so often in the dream, in all of his dreams these days, no matter what is going on there is Linc's 'Slap!' in his dreams.

And down the street, a little while later, the sound of a car door slamming sounds like that 'slap!' in Thyme's pill-induced dream. (He's dreaming about her, Chastity, in her t-shirt and socks, and nothing else, and he dreams she's on the beach, by herself, and takes off her socks, and then she takes off her shirt, and she's walking up the beach naked, but Thyme, in his dream, is far behind her, and he can't really see her naked, until she turns and starts to walk towards him, and then, all of a sudden in his dream he has his camera with him and he tries to take a picture of her, but it jams, and then the dream ends. And then the dream starts over again.)

And down the street, that sound of that car door slamming sounds like nothing to Chastity, spaced out in her hazy-blue noise. (She's dreaming she's walking around at the beach, in a t-shirt and shorts, walking up and the down the beach holding the hand of a little girl, who's smiling and laughing, and Chastity keeps looking into the surf for a body, she keeps looking at the breakers to see her mother floating away, but she never sees one, and she smiles as she walks on the sand.)

This is ten minutes later, and this is how it is:

The car door slams (Slap!); Stan gets out of his car.

He looks around and heads to the empty house across the street from Chastity's. He walks around to the back of the house, he walks likes he's supposed to be there, like he lives there, but there is no one watching.

He walks around in the shadows, does nothing for about ten minutes, and then goes to the side of the house, behind a bush, in the dark, and he watches the house, Chastity's house, and he sees the blue light downstairs, and he sees it's dark everywhere else, and he watches, and he sees no signs of life, no movement, and he stands still behind the bush for ten minutes.

He takes gloves from his pocket, and puts them on.

Then, he walks down the driveway, pauses at the sidewalk, glances around, acting casually, and walks across the street and right up Chastity's driveway, past her car, and turns right onto the sidewalk, and walks up to the door.

Stan stands at the front door for a minute, then two. He puts his ear to the door. He smells the air.

He puts his hand on the door handle.

He holds it there, for a minute, then two.

Then he turns his wrist. And the knob moves.

It's unlocked. Chastity forgot to lock it; she didn't think she'd be stoned-out on the sofa that early; Thyme had assumed that Chastity would lock the doors.

It's unlocked.

Stan turns the knob, and holds the door closed, and holds the handle unhinged for a minute, then two.

And then he opens the door a little, three inches, then four, and he holds it, and listens but he hears nothing, and he sees nothing but the hazy-blue, and then he opens it two inches more, then three and pauses, and then after a minute, then two, he opens it so he can slip his whole body in, and he comes into the house, into Chastity's house: he enters the hazy-blue house.

He stands in the hall for a minute, two. He smells the pot; he sees the hazy-blue. He feels at peace for a minute. He takes his gloves off.

And then he walks into Chastity's living room, where she's asleep on the sofa, and he stares at her for a minute, then two, and he looks down and sees where she laid the joint she was smoking, and he picks it up. The joint is out, and he puts it into his pocket, and he stares at her for a minute, then two. He takes a step forward, and he bends over, towards her navel, towards where the t-shirt stopped, and he breathes deeply through his nose, and he can smell her. He stops, looks at her eyes closed eyes, then her breasts, and he walks out of the living room, and into the hallway. He can still smell her.

He listens: all quiet.

He walks into the kitchen. He opens and closes two drawers and finally finds a rolling pin and he pulls it out and stares at it for a minute, then two.

He walks back into the hallway and goes up the staircase. He looks into the first bedroom and it's empty, and then he opens the next door and at first all he sees are a lot of books everywhere, and then he looks onto the floor and he sees Thyme, bearded and seemingly passed out, fully dressed, on his back.

Stan stands there with the rolling pin in his hand and glares at Thyme for a minute, then two.

His nostrils start to bleed, both of them, but the left one starts first.

He touches his face, above his mouth, and his fingers are red with blood. He stares at Thyme; he glares at him.

He holds the rolling pin in his left hand, and wipes blood from his nostrils with his right hand.

Thyme sleeps. Soundly.

Stan stares. Steadily.

Stan gets some blood on his fingers and smears it onto the rolling pin and then lays it next to Thyme, on his sleeping bag.

Stan spits on Thyme, and then leaves the room.

Stan goes back down the stairs and he goes into the room where Chastity is sleeping on the sofa, and he picks up the remote control and he puts it in his pocket. He stands over her, and he bends down again, he's almost resting his head in her lap, and he smells her, for a minute, two. And he puts the remote control down, and he lifts up her shirt a little bit, she begins to snore, and he can see her, all of her, and he bends down and smells her. He reaches down and touches her pubic hair, then grabs the remote control, stands up, and leaves the room.

In the hallway, he pauses and he puts his gloves back on, and he hears nothing, and he closes the door behind him, making sure to lock the handle this time, not as it was earlier, and he walks away from the door, down the sidewalk, down the driveway, and then walks in the empty street to his car. He opens the door and slams it (Slap!) and starts the car and then drives off.

And in his dreams, all Thyme heard was Linc's 'Slap!' and he slept, soundly.

Slap!, even in his dreams; even in his dreams, Slap!

Chapter Thirty-five

A Slap in the Face

This is the next morning, now, and this is how it is:

Thyme wakes up and goes back to sleep without getting up or looking around, and he drifts off to sleep for a few minutes and then he wakes up again, blinks his eyes, looks towards the windows to see how light it is outside, rubs his eyes, and coughs.

He sits up and lifts his knees up and then rests his head on his knees, closing his eyes for a minute. Then he's ready to stand up.

He puts his left hand down on the floor next to the sleeping bag and then lowers his right hand and finds the rolling pin: "What?"

He lifts it up and looks at it.

He isn't so sure he didn't put it there, sleepwalking or something. He doesn't realize that that's blood on it, real blood, Stan's blood.

He stares at it for a minute, then two. And then he gets up and walks over to the window and stares out the window for a minute, then two.

He turns and walks out of the room, down the hall, and then down the stairs. At the bottom of the steps he checks the front door and finds the handle locked.

He walks past the living room and Chastity is still sleeping on the couch; Thyme is holding the bloodied rolling pin in his hand. After a minute, maybe two, Chastity wakes up, startled by bearded Thyme hovering near her with a rolling pin.

"What's that?"

"A rolling pin."

"What's on it?"

"I don't know; it looks like blood."

"Is it yours? The blood?"

Thyme scratched his beard and looks down at the rolling pin, "I don't think so."

"Why do you have it? What time is it?"

"I don't know, and I don't know."

She looks over at the television, "Hand me the remote and I'll put it on a news channel so we can see the time." She puts her hands behind the cushions, Thyme looks around the room, and then he bends down and looks under the sofa.

"I don't see it anywhere," he says.

She finds a lighter under a cushion and looks over to the ashtray, thinking about relighting the joint she never finished last night. It's not there. She looks on the floor.

"Did you start smoking again?"

"No," he says, "Why?"

"No reason. So why do you have that rolling pin, again?"

"That's what I'm trying to figure out. It was on my sleeping bag next to me when I woke up today."

Chastity has gotten up off of the sofa now, she's on her hands and knees going around the room looking for either the remote control or her joint, or both, whatever she can find.

Thyme stares at the blue screen; Chastity walks over to the television and manually changes the channel, not to a cable news channel, but to one of the local channels that is talking about the morning weather and the rush hour commute.

Chastity looks over at Thyme and says, "It's seven thirty."

Thyme nods his head and says nothing for a minute, then two, and finally says, "I think someone was in here last night."

A few minutes later, as Thyme comes back in the room munching on some leftover bacon for breakfast and Chastity is rolling herself a new joint for the morning, the local news comes back from a commercial break.

The newscaster starts the news segment with the following: "This station has just been given details on the body found in the foreclosed house on Maplewood Avenue earlier this week. A police report states that the body of Erin Patterson, a 35 year old female, was found inside the house. The report gives no cause of death, but states that Patterson did not live in the house, and that no one else was found in the house. Police say a realtor called in that evening after having dropped by the house to take pictures. Patterson was employed as a manager at a local grocery store. As, and if, more details in this story emerge we'll have full coverage here. Next up . . ."

Click.

Chastity turns the television off.

She sits on the sofa wordless.

Thyme sits on the floor, with his back to the wall, and stares ahead at nothing, and they are silent.

"I'm going to have to tell Linc I quit."

"Quit what? You don't have a job."

"Oh. Good point."

"Don't worry about it; go. Help your friend. I'll keep the baseball bat close."

Slap!

It's the end of the day; Thyme is still on the back of the truck.

(Linc is driving, but not because his foot's still hurt; he's driving because Thyme drove thru one stop sign and one red light, both times almost getting Linc hit off the back of the truck by the oncoming traffic.

"I'm driving. What, are you stoned?"

"What?"

"What's wrong with you, man?"

"Nothing; we'll talk about it later."

"Still, I'm driving, get to the back.")

Slap!

The truck stops.

Thyme hops off the back and walks to the passenger's door and opens it, climbs in, and slams it behind him.

"God I'm tired."

"Yeah, driving this thing is a lot nicer than hauling those cans." Linc has an unlit cigarette behind his ear; it's been there all day. Thyme's thinking about grabbing it and smoking it.

"Someone was in the house last night."

"Last night?" Linc looks over towards Thyme: "Who?"

"It's got to be him."

"Did you see him?"

"No. I was knocked out."

"Chastity?"

"No. Stoned out, sleeping."

"You think it was him though?"

"Got to be. He left a rolling pin next to me."

"Yeah?"

"With blood on it."

"Yeah? No fooling?"

"No fooling, my friend, no fooling."

Linc drives on silently.

"Well, I'm going to come and stay there for a while."

"You don't need to do that."

"Do you need a slap in the face? Of course I do." He stops at a light and fingers the unlit cigarette behind his ear, "You two are my friends."

"Thanks, Linc."

Slap!

That night, Linc and Thyme park the truck behind a convenience store, and go inside and buy two coffees and give the manager a twenty dollar bill and asks him not to tow the truck and he can keep the change, and then they walk about seven blocks to Chastity's house.

It's later that night, and this is how it is: Thyme has two pills in his hand. He's about to swallow them down, waterless, and Linc walks by and wraps his tattooed hand around Thyme's forearm.

"What is that, man?"

"Nothing, Linc."

"No. What is that?"

"Just a couple pills. To help me sleep. They help. Some."

Linc just looks at Thyme and then shakes his head back and forth. "Yeah, it helps so much you don't notice someone putting a bloody rolling pin next to you."

"I sleep better."

"On the floor."

"Feels like feathers."

Chastity enters the kitchen and starts looking around. She opens all the cabinets, but takes nothing out of any of them, leaving them all open. She lifts herself up onto the countertop, and she sits there, facing out.

Linc looks over at her and says, "I'm staying here tonight."

"Good. You're cooking."

"Fine. We're having spaghetti. You got meat?"

"No."

"Mushrooms."

"No. Neither kind," she smiles.

"Spaghetti sauce?"

"Tomato paste."

"Good enough. I can make that work. You do have some spaghetti in here, right?"

Chastity stares at him, smiles, "Hopefully."

Thyme puts the sleeping pills back into his pocket; he wasn't planning on eating, he wanted to go to bed, but he's started to get a little hungry. He sits on the sofa; it feels good to sit down. He turns on the television; it's already tuned to the news. Wars. Foreclosures. The war on drugs in Latin America, the war on drugs in Mexico, the war on drugs in Chastity's kitchen, where the pasta is boiling and the drugs, apparently, are winning.

Linc drops some spaghetti into the boiling water; Chastity finds oregano, garlic salt, thyme.

Thyme starts to zone out; so Chastity decides to start to zone out and she lights up a joint; and Linc hits it and zones out and says "Twenty minutes" and no one responds but everyone hears him and then it's quiet for twenty minutes, twenty two minutes, and then Linc says, "Dinner's ready."

Thyme eats on the sofa, in front of the television, watching the news; he falls asleep during a segment on personal bankruptcy. The sleeping pills are still in his pocket; he's just exhausted.

Chastity stays up and smokes half of another joint with Linc, who's sitting on the second stair leading up, directly facing the front door. He's got a golf club between his knees, his father's unlit cigarette behind his right ear; he's staring at the front door. Chastity smokes half with Linc, and then leaves him in his guard-dog mode, and drags herself back to the sofa, lifts up Thyme's feet and then sits down and puts them onto her lap. She's still smoking her joint; she hits it again, watching the news and not paying attention, and it falls and burns Thyme's ankles, sockless above the edge of his dirty sneakers, and that wakes him up for a second to look around the room startled and cuss a little; and then he smiles and falls back asleep, a small blister forming on his ankle. Chastity smokes and watches the show; listeners are calling in and talking to the show's hosts about their 401(k), government bonds, and other things Chastity doesn't have. And she snubs out her joint and tries to keep her eyes open but she can't and she falls asleep, leaning down onto Thyme, and using his legs as a cover.

Thyme dreams that he's driving a red car, which becomes blue after a turn he takes too fast, and he's being pulled over by a policeman on a motorcycle; and Thyme pulls the car over; and the policeman walks up and takes off his helmet and it turns out that the policeman is Momma, and Thyme tries to talk to Momma, it is her, right there outside the window of Chastity's car that Thyme is now driving, was speeding in; but Momma ignores him; when she talks, she has the voice of a man; and she pulls out a pad and starts to write him a ticket, and she tells him, in a man's voice, to slow down and take it easy, and she never smiles at him; she writes him a ticket and she puts her helmet back on and walks back to the motorcycle and gets on and pulls off. Thyme looks down at his ticket that Momma gave him; the fine is three pennies; and all that Momma wrote on the ticket, while lecturing him in a man's voice, was 'Thyme's Passing' over and over and over. And he's in the car, and looking at the ticket, wondering if Momma will come back to give him another ticket, and outside of the car window he hears a Slap!

Slap!, even in his dreams; even in his dreams, Slap!

And on the stairs, Lincoln is snoring.
 Down the block, a car door closes.
 Slap!

Chapter Thirty-six

It Already Feels Like Something

This is the middle of the night, now, and this is how it is:

She woke up first. Thyme's awake at the other end of the couch; their legs are touching.

Warmth.

Eye contact.

She is wearing socks and a long t-shirt, and nothing else.

Thyme is looking at Chastity as she is not paying attention and she moves her legs around not even thinking about what she's doing; Thyme sees that all Chastity is wearing is a t-shirt and socks.

She rolled a joint before she started to speak, and he smiled and handed her the closest lighter, and she lights up and then starts:

"I guess I've never wanted to have kids. I never pretended my dolls were my daughters. I never wanted to have sex because I knew that if I did, it would happen. You know. I didn't want to have a kid to grow up feeling like me. Accidental. I guess I felt that was as a kid, and then as a teenager, and then when I grew up, if I've ever grown up, I was just stuck." She pauses, smiles, rubs his leg a little and then her own a little, all the while hitting the joint and exhaling out her nose, coughing and choking, then putting it down, after first extending it in offering to Thyme, who shakes his head no, and smiles.

She goes on: "And with all the stuff in the world, all the crazy stuff that happens, and here I am hung up about something that doesn't really matter. It's dumb."

"No, it's not. It means something to you."

"Yeah, but it's still stupid; that after all these years, and I'm looking back on it now twenty-five years later, and I see me then, pent-up, frustrated, passed around, and I was just lost, so lost." She pauses, tears in her eyes; she reaches for the joint and picks it up and then immediately puts it back into

the ashtray. She smiles a little through tears towards Thyme and says with
a shake, "I just felt so lost all the time, just numbingly lost."

"I see."

"And it's dumb, it's so dumb that I let that affect me all these years;
I mean, look at what's going on; AIDs, Africa, not to mention all the
stuff since 9/11, and here I was bothered about something that happened
in the seventies, being left by my parents in the seventies; then in the
eighties, I was old enough to really have issues; I had no friends, just
issues, problems. Problems with myself. I guess that's never stopped."
She reaches down and picks up the joint and puts it up to her lips, and
she inhales, deeply she inhales, and she holds her breath, and she hold
it so long that she turns a little red; she exhales, holds in a cough, and
says, "I already feel like something now; I already feel like something
new now. New, now."

He rubs her leg now; Linc snores on the steps.

Thyme says to her: "You look good; I mean, you look like you feel good
now, better. And you do look good."

She put her hand on his hand, which is on her leg.

"Are you working tomorrow?"

He rubs his beard, says: "You know I don't have a job. But no, I don't
think so; not tomorrow."

"Good. Let's sleep late, here on this sofa."

"Okay."

"Give me one of those unemployment pills."

"Unemployment pills?"

"The ones in your pocket; the white ones."

Thyme pulls out a sleeping pill and gives it to Chastity; she swallows
it without water, and then Thyme pulls one from his pocket and does the
same.

She looks down at the joint on the table; sees it is almost out, but still
smoking a little, and she asks Thyme: "You want to kill that?"

"I'll sleep all night anyway."

"Better dreams."

"Okay." Thyme picks up the dying joint, doesn't relight it, but hits it
hard, and the end turns red and his lungs fill up with sweetly dirty smoke
and his throat burns and he can feel his pulse in his temple, and he tries to
fight off a cough, but he can't, and he coughs, he coughs the biggest cough
he's coughed in months, and his lungs burn, and he puts the joint down,
and he wipes water from his eyes and feels the need to both spit and drink

something, and he coughs a little more, and then a little more, and finally he says, "That's right, that's right; I remember now."

They don't speak for a minute, then two, and she reaches over and touches him gently on his hand, his bad hand, and she says to him, "Good night; I'm so sorry that I shot you."

"Good night; I'm glad you shot me."

In a little while, they're both sound asleep thanks to the unemployment pills.

Slap!, even in his dreams; even in his dreams, Slap!

Linc wakes up and doesn't move much; his eyes open, he licks his lips. He's concentrating. Using his fingers and doing math; he's adding up the time that Thyme's been helping him, and he adds up what the pay would be, pulls out his wallet, and fishes around in there for the money (he'd been planning on doing this for a while) and stuffs the bills into his shirt pocket, and then stands up on the stairs and walks up.

At the top of the stairs, he turns and walks down the hall, then turn into the library, where he sees Thyme's empty sleeping bag. He walks over to the desk, pulls out the desk chair so he can get to the center drawer, opens in, and puts the cash into the drawer. He closes the desk drawer, and then walks over to the books, and he sees one of Momma's books, and he sits down on Thyme's sleeping bag, and begins to read *Time's Passing*.

The car door had closed (Slap!), down the street, about two hours ago. It is cold out, but not below freezing and Stan is patient.

He walks past empty house after empty house on the opposite side of the street from Chastity's house. He has a ski hat on, a scarf, gloves; he walks at ease, like he does this every night. He walks like a man who's supposed to be on this deserted street, at one thirty a.m., in thirty-five degree temperature, with no flashlight, just a key chain, his cell phone, the television remote control, a book of matches (with six matches left), and Chastity's partially smoked joint in his coat pocket.

He walks past Chastity's house at first, he walks past the house where Erin's body was found, and he pauses, and pulls out his cell phone and takes a picture of the dark, empty house.

He stands there for a couple of minutes, then turns around and walks back a little. In the distant a dog barks, not too close, but Stan checks behind him, slows down just a bit to look less suspicious, and then turns left into the driveway of the house he hid out behind last time.

He does the same thing again; he goes in the back and takes a piss, spits, zips up, and then goes and stands at the back corner of the house, near the driveway, behind a big trash can, and he stares across the street towards Chastity's house.

He sees the library light come on, and stay on, and he watches for a few minutes until he's sure that whoever is up there is going to stay. He walks down the driveway, casually, like he's getting his morning paper, pauses at the edge of the street, it's all dark and quiet up and down the street, the only light is the one upstairs in Chastity's house, where Linc is on the floor on Thyme's sleeping bag, reading.

Stan crosses the street.

He stops at the edge of the driveway, and then walks past the car, around the side of the house to a window, one he's looked in before, and in the dim light, he can make out the sofa and he can see two people sleeping on it. He stares into the darkness, waiting for his eyes to adjust.

He pulls the joint and the book of matches from his pocket. Three matches die before he finally holds the last three together as one and lights them at the same time, and he holds the joint over the matches until the end catches fire, then holds it upright for a minute before blowing out the flame at the end and holding the joint up to his lips he takes a violent hit, and then holds his breathe, exhales, and then continues with much smaller hits, smoking and staring at the sofa, staring at the two sleeping bodies.

He can't be more than nine feet away; the curtain is open a little, he can see better now, thanks to the darkness, the adjustment, and the pot. At least, he feels he can see better now.

He takes his last hit on the joint and drops it down onto the grass and dead leaves at his feet; it fizzles out from the night's moisture. He puts his right hand into his pants pocket and rubs himself gently.

He stops rubbing himself, but keeps his hand on himself and continues to stare into the window.

With his left hand, he pulls the remote control from his pocket; and with his right hand he pulls his cell phone from the other pocket.

Through the window, into the darkness, he takes a picture with his cell phone, the flash goes off, but he doesn't care, his blood is running too fast. The phone clicks, whizzes; he looks at the picture, it's much clearer than what he can see without the flash.

Then he lifts the remote control up to the window and turns on the television, the volume is low. He finds a different channel, not the news channel, but a cartoon channel. The volume is low; the room is awash in the psychedelic glow of the cartoon. Then Stan starts to increase the volume on the television, still holding the remote control up with his left hand and the cell phone up with his right.

The volume started at '0' on the bottom of the screen, then went up to '7', then '12', then '23', then '35' and still the bodies on the sofa did not move until he hit '42' and at that point Chastity sleepily staggers towards the television and the whole time Stan is capturing this on video on the cell phone through the window, as Chastity, in only socks and the t-shirt, runs over towards the television, ass hanging out, and turns down the volume but keeps the picture on, and then she turns around and facing Stan lifts up her t-shirt to rub her eyes with it and Stan and his cell phone are left staring at her pubic hair, her belly button, and her breasts. Then she goes back to the sofa and lies down again; Thyme does not move at all.

Stan can almost smell her.

In the darkness, in the cold, he rubs himself, and he holds up the remote control again to the window, with his cell phone in the other hand, and he starts to increase the volume again. It gets louder and he gets harder and he puts the cell phone away and just holds the remote control in one hand and rubs himself with his other hand, and the volume goes to '15' and then to '25' and then to '39' and at that point Stan hears the front door to the house slam and hears a booming voice shout, "I'm going to stuff this golf club inside you!"

And Stan turns and runs into the backyard right before Linc turns to corner of the house, with a golf club in one hand, and the bloodied rolling pin in the other. Stan runs into the backyard of the house next door, and hides behind the shed in the far corner of the yard.

Linc spends the next twenty minutes walking patrol outside of Chastity's house, talking loudly to no one saying, "First thing I'll do is slip this Nine Iron up inside of you, you tampon-eater. I know you're out here; I'm just waiting for you. I'm going to get you, you perverted-pansy. The second thing I'm going do is smash your pale balls with this rolling pin, you father-sucker."

Linc keeps walking around the house and talking; Stan hears him; Stan is scared. Stan hasn't seen any flashlight beams and suspects Linc may be in the dark without a light.

With Linc still yelling in the yard, Stan pulls out his cell phone, and after looking around and seeing that he is sufficiently out of view, he turns on the phone and watches the video of Chastity. He watches it again, the two minute video of everything he's wanted to see on her, of her bare ass running across the room, he wants to lick it, and when she turned and wiped the sleep from her eyes with her shirt, it was a dream come true, and on the third time watching the video, without even touching himself, Stan is in ecstasy.

And in the background, he can hear Linc yelling out death threats, and his crotch is wet, and it tingles, and he watches his video again, and then again, and finally he hears Linc stop yelling, and the front door close, and it's quiet, and Stan watches the video one more time, and then, snake that he is, slithers away from Chastity's house, taking a long detour around the block back to his car, gets in (Slap!), and in the dark he watches the video again before he turns his car on and drives home, where he watches the video again, and again.

In the morning, Linc goes outside in the light and walks around the house. He pauses at the window looking in to the television, and sees the trampled grass, and he bends down to look closer and he finds the burnt out joint on the ground and he picks it up and takes it inside to show Chastity and Thyme.

This is that day, today, and this is how it is: Thyme didn't go with Linc today; he slept late on the sofa, and then woke up and cooked some bacon for Chastity. Chastity has unplugged the television and made a makeshift curtain on the window out of a quilt.

The bacon burns a little; grease spits out of the frying pan and lands on Thyme's filthy tennis shoes. He smiles: it'll make them smell better. He drains grease down the sink; he thinks of Momma, and how she always would get after him for doing that, how she'd always skillfully pour the hot grease from the pan into an empty wine bottle nestled just right in the trashcan. He remembers the bacon Momma would make for him; just a little burnt, a little black, just like he likes it.

Chastity is walking around the house, going from window to window, making sure they are locked. She's closing all the blinds, and pulling curtains closed.

Thyme turns off the stove burner, puts the frying pan down on a cold burner, and then he leaves the kitchen, goes up the stairs, and he comes back down in less than a minute with his camera dangling around his neck.

"I'm going outside," and he opens the front door and walks out. He turns the corner past the driveway and goes around to the window where

Linc had found the joint this morning in the dew, the grass in the grass, and Thyme stands there, at that window, just thinking. From there, he takes a picture of the faint foot prints in the grass. Thyme follows the steps through the yard, into the yard next door, another empty house, and he walks to the shed. He goes around the corner of the shed and notices where the grass was pushed down from Stan the night before, and he takes a picture of the area. He stands there for a minute, then two; then he follows the steps though another yard until they end at a sidewalk and, left without a trail, Thyme turns and walks back to the shed, then to Chastity's backyard, and then to the window, and then back inside through the front door, where the smell of bacon brought him back into the warmth of the house and made his stomach rumble. He walks into the kitchen, where Chastity is, and he walks up behind her, his camera is around his neck and bumping, gently but coldly, into Chastity's back.

After some bacon, Thyme walks back out the front door, and for the first time in weeks, since Momma's house burnt down, he hears those dog tags clinking together in the yard, and he smiles, and says to the empty air next to him: "I was wondering where you've been."

It's later that day, and this is how it is:

Linc opens the front door with the key Chastity had given him (the doors stay locked all night and all day recently), and he comes in, wordlessly, and sits on the empty sofa. Thyme's on the floor, his back against the wall, reading one of his mother's books; Chastity is wandering aimlessly around the room, doing nothing.

Linc coughs a little, rubs his nose, and says to Thyme, "I saw your mother today?"

"You saw Momma?"

"I did. I swear. It was weird."

"Yeah, I've seen her; so has Chastity."

"She was just standing there, at a stop sign on a corner, and she was just staring at me."

"Smiling?"

"No."

"Frowning?"

"No."

"Hmm."

"Yeah."

Chastity says, "I saw her on television, on a cooking show once; she knew my name."

Linc goes on, "Maybe next time I should try to talk to her?"

Thyme asks, "What would you say?"

"I guess I'd say, 'Tell my Pops that I miss him.'"

"Sometimes, I wonder if my mom is dead," Chastity's speaking aloud to Thyme and Linc; they're on the front porch, in sweaters, drinking cans of beer; it's turned unseasonably warm as the day went on. The sun is almost down; Linc and Thyme down their beers. "I wonder if my dad is dead. I could have walked past their graves in the cemetery and not even known it; I could have stumbled over her grave and not even known. Maybe I should try to talk to Momma the next time I see her; ask her if she's seen my parents."

Thyme asks, "What if she asks their names?"

"I don't know if names are as important on the other side as they are here."

Linc asks, "What if she asks what they look like?"

"I'll just say that I bet they look a lot like me . . . or that I look a lot like them."

Thyme asks, "What if she said that they're not there, that they're here, alive."

"What if?"

Linc asks, "Would you look for them?"

"I doubt they'd want me to. No one wants a thirty-year-old baby-girl . . . with issues." She smiles.

Linc goes on, "Seems to me, after me losing Pop, and with Thyme's Momma dying and all, it just seems to me if you had the chance to find your mom, well, I think I'd do it."

Thyme says, "Not me. I bet my dad is alive, but that doesn't mean I need him or even want contact with him, and I doubt that he's been sitting around almost three and a half decades wondering when I'm going to send him a birthday party invitation. I bet he doesn't even know I exist; if he did, he's forgotten about me, and intentionally I'd say."

Linc says, "But, you're part of him; he's part of you."

"Just because he slept with my mom doesn't mean a whole lot to me; that rottingbrain Stan Thimbleshit slept with my mom, and we're not exactly endeared to each other."

Chastity speaks, "I agree, Thyme. Nature is nature. Reproduction. The birds and the bees, but that has nothing to do with me."

Inside now, a little later, Chastity asks to Linc, "What happened to your mother?"

"She died, years ago, when I was in high school. In a car wreck. She was on medication, and had a drink or two, and decided that she needed to go to the store, and decided to go to the store across the river. She missed the bridge completely; her car went down a steep hill and landed on some rocks. But no one saw it, or at least no one stopped. The next morning some joggers found her. Dying, but not dead. She died later that morning."

A little later still, Linc asks to Chastity, "What if you found out you had a brother? Or a sister?"

She's silent for a minute, then two, then answers, "If it came down to I just had a brother, or a sister, and we take parents out of the equation, I'd be thrilled. I think I'd try to find them; I think I would find them; I know I would find them." She stops talking for a minute, then two, stares at the wall, with a smile on her face, "Yes. Yes. I think I would find them, and I think it would be good, would feel good; in fact, it already feels like, oh I don't know, but it feels like something."

And she doesn't speak for an hour; she just sits there, smiling, and she's not even stoned.

Later, she stops smiling, and speaks softly to Thyme: "I already feel good; better. It's funny how you get so mad about something for so long, and then meet people, friends, and they can ask you these simple questions, and it's like a new light, a new life, a new feeling; what if I had a sister? And then I thought about it for a little while, and I thought, what if I had more than a sister. What if I had a daughter? I mean, I've always tried to talk myself out of it for stupid reasons; I've always hated the idea of parents because I never had parents. For once, I don't want to feel so alone, not all alone. I hate having things, and not having somebody."

They all dream that night:

Chastity dreams that she's on the beach again, in the same t-shirt and shorts, and the water is calmer, the sky is clear, it's sunny but she doesn't feel hot; she holding the hand of a child, a little boy this time, and he looks a little like her, and he's running around in sandy diapers, and the water is calm, and she still looks into the waves for her mother to be floating around, but she doesn't see her. She smiles, and she feels better, good even.

Linc dreams that he gets home from work, after dropping Thyme off, and grabs the mail and he's opening the checks from his customers and he opens one that has Momma's burnt down address as the return address, and he opens it, and it's a check dated just two days ago, for trash service, and it's signed by Suzanne, and the memo section simply says 'thanks!' and then he wakes up and when he falls asleep again he starts to dream about the waitress at the bar.

Thyme dreams that he's working at the store, when Momma was still alive, and Erin was still alive, and Thyme was barefoot, and employed, a little at least. He's putting small glass containers of olives onto the shelves, he's got boxes and boxes of olives near him; Erin walks down the aisle, wearing her name tag and clipboard and alive and working, and she's walks up to Thyme and says words that she's said to him before, 'I've had dreams at night about him, bad dreams,' and then she walks off, and Thyme keeps on working in his dream, and then she comes down the aisle again, and repeats everything again, like she didn't just come down, she walks up time and time again to Thyme and says 'I've had dreams at night about him, bad dreams,' and Thyme hears it over and over again, sitting there, stocking olives.

Stan dreams about Erin, in her house, alive, and he dreams he's walking up to her front door, and he opens it, and he walks in, and it's a bad dream in a good way, or a good dream in a bad way, and in the dream he really enjoyed it, but Erin did not.

Chapter Thirty-seven

Indecent Exposure, Underemployment, and No Laughter

This is the next day, now, and this is how it is:

Thyme did not go to Erin's funeral; he missed it, being too preoccupied with Stan and Chastity, and helping Linc when he could. But that's nothing new for Thyme; he's always missing final farewells; he's told himself to go, to do it and get there, but he's not strong enough. He's missed all of the important funerals in his life; he's sure the only one he'll make it to will be his own.

He wants to go see Erin's grave; take a picture of it; leave some flowers. He has his camera with him, and in his right hand he has some plastic flowers; the flowers were given to him the other day by the manager at the grocery store; Erin had these fake flowers on her desk for years. He cleaned the dust off today.

Thyme also has a travel mug full of hot yerba matte tea.

He and Chastity leave the house, dead bolting the front door behind them, and they get into her car. At first it doesn't start; on the third try, and after letting it sit for a few minutes, the ignition finally turns and Chastity lets it run for a minute, then two, before backing out.

She pauses before she actually pulls out into the street and looks both ways, then backs out and says to Thyme (although not actually looking towards him), "I don't know why I even bother to look. This neighborhood is dead; has been dead for a while." Thyme doesn't say anything; she thinks for a few seconds and then says, "Well, I guess that wasn't the best choice of phrases, seeing where we're going."

"It's okay."

"Sorry."

"It's okay; don't worry about it." He stares out the window and then smiles over towards her, "I remember my old friend used to have a couple dogs, and one he had for years and years; Royal, that was his name: Royal. The other dog was a stray that had basically adopted my friend; that dog was called Brown. He was brown. Anyway, one day Royal died; it had been coming for a long time, the dog was fourteen or so. The thing is, all the years that Royal was alive, I kept on forgetting his name; I'd call him King or Prince or even Brown. For some reason I could never get it right; maybe it was all the drugs we were on. Then, after Royal died, whenever I went over to visit Tony, that was my friend, I'd always call Brown by the wrong name; I'd say 'Come here Royal; good Royal; I have a treat for Royal.' And Brown would just look at me, and Tony would get all quiet, I know it bothered him, but it happened time after time; I could never get it right . . ."

"Maybe it was the drugs you were on."

"Maybe; maybe I have a thick head."

"Maybe."

They drive on in silence.

When they enter the cemetery, Chastity pulls up in front of the office and Thyme gets out and goes in; less than five minutes later, he's back in the car with a map. "She's over there," pointing to his left, "But, if you don't mind, I want to go visit Momma first, for a minute."

She drives the opposite way from Erin's grave, to where Momma is; she stops and asks Thyme, "Do you want to go alone?"

"Do you mind if I do?"

"Of course not."

Thyme gets out, leaving his camera and Erin's plastic flowers in the car, and he walks to Momma's grave carrying the travel mug full of warm yerba matte.

Chastity watches Thyme standing there, in front of Momma's headstone, looking down. After a few minutes of silence, he bends down and kisses Momma's headstone and leaves the travel mug sitting there, then turns around and walks back to the car.

He gets in; wipes tears from his eyes.

Chastity wipes a tear from his bearded cheek and asks, "You okay?"

"No. Let's go. That way."

She moves her hand from his cheek and turns the car back on.

In a few minutes, they find Erin's gravesite. It's easy to find; it's the only freshly dug grave in an area of older ones.

Chastity gets out, carrying Thyme's camera, and Thyme gets out, carrying Erin's flowers. They walk, side by side, to the gravesite; and stand there. Chastity takes a picture of the headstone with the new dirt below it; Thyme bends down and places the plastic flowers on the headstone, and then Chastity takes another picture.

They stand in silence for a moment.

Chastity looks over to Thyme, and takes his hand in hers, and asks, "Have you ever contacted the police?"

"About what?"

"Erin."

"Erin?"

"And Stan. Don't you think Stan killed her?"

"I don't know; I think so; but I don't know."

"And your house? Don't you think that Stan did that, too?"

"I'm not sure, I think so; calling the police just isn't my thing."

They're silent. They stand and look at the grave for a few minutes.

"Don't you think you should call the police?"

He's silent.

She continues, "For her. For Erin. She was your friend."

He nods, "Yeah. You're right. She was my friend. I'll call the police tomorrow, after Linc and I are done."

"Good." And she squeezes his hand and they turn and walk back to her car, get in, turn the car on, and drive away from Erin.

Going towards the office, that brick building in the middle of the graves, Chastity takes a turn and heads back towards Momma's grave.

"Why?"

"I need to say goodbye, too, Thyme."

She twists at five miles per hour through the deserted cemetery and leaves the car in the same place as when she waited for Thyme.

She walks over and after a minute, while she's looking down to the grave, she hears a car door shut, and Thyme gets out and walks over.

"It's gone."

"What?"

"The tea."

"Maybe a caretaker took it, thinking it was left by mistake; maybe it's in the office."

"Maybe."

"Thyme, put your hand in my pocket. The right one."

He does; he pulls his hand out and opens his palm and there are three pennies. He gives two to Chastity, and keeps the other for himself. They walk over, simultaneously, without consulting each other, and place their pennies onto Momma's headstone. Thyme places his one first, and then Chastity places hers on top of his.

Then, they turn and walk back to the car: Chastity, a virgin, not an angel, and Thyme, a bearded skinny skeleton.

The car starts on the third try again, and they drive off.

"Linc's not going to be over tonight."

"Is he mad at you?"

"Mad at me? Why?"

"For not working for him as much recently."

"He understands. Besides, it's not my job. I think he has a date. He is, as he says, the trash man, baby; baby, he's the trash man," Thyme stops and smiles and rubs his beard, "He'll be by in the morning for me."

Three blocks from home, Thyme, wordlessly, reaches over and taps Chastity's shoulder, getting her attention, and she turns, and not a half block away, they see Momma, standing there, staring in their direction, in the cold, alone, and holding the travel mug of tea that Thyme left for her. She's looking at them but not making eye contact; she's not smiling, but not frowning, she's just looking at them, and all they can do it stare back, stare back at Momma on the street corner lost in a thousand yard stare. Steam is rising from the tea mug, but she never lifts the mug up to drink it; steam is rising in the cold winter air, but no steam is coming out from Momma's mouth.

Suddenly, and still without blinking or taking her gaze from them, she turns and starts to walk off.

By the time Chastity and Thyme reach where she is, not twenty seconds later, she's gone: nowhere in sight.

Later that night, Thyme takes a sleeping pill and sinks into oblivion on the sofa as Chastity sits on the other end and smokes a joint, watching the news, and in a way she's waiting for Momma to appear on the news and start talking to Chastity about the events of the day, the economy, underemployment, foreclosures, and crime in the city.

But she never does.

Now it's now, two hours later, and this is how it is: Stan parks his car (Slap!) down the street and walks in front of Chastity's house and stands there. The house is quiet; the only light is the flicker of the television through the window. The whole street is quiet; Stan looks up and down the street and doesn't see any lights on in any of the houses; he knows that they are empty.

It's cold; he shoves his hands in his pocket.

He walks over to Chastity's car and tries to open the driver's door, but it's locked. He looks up at the house, sees no one in the windows, and then he unzips the fly on his pants, pulls himself out, and urinates on the driver's door handle. He spits on the window.

He walks backwards out of the yard, and crosses the street; he goes behind the house across the street from Chastity's. He's been here before and he knows that it's empty. He walks around back. The last two times that he was here, he's seen a brick, and he goes and picks it up and walks to the back door, the one that is locked by the handle but not by a deadbolt. He smashes the pane next to the handle, carefully reaches in, unlocks the door, and then looks around to make sure no one has seen him; he laughs to himself: there is no one to see him. He lets himself in. The house is dark and cold, but it's right across the street from where he wants to be, and it's warmer inside than outside.

He goes upstairs to the second floor, and into the front bedroom; he opens the blinds enough to see out, but not all the way; Chastity's house across the street is still dark. He watches for a minute, then two.

Finally, he turns around and puts his back to the wall, squatting down.

He takes his cell phone from his jacket pocket and turns on the power, it's now the only light in the house. He watches the video he made of Chastity the other day. He watches it again. And then he unzips his pants, and watches the video again, and again, and again.

This is the next morning, now, and this is how it is:

Thyme wakes up on the sofa; Chastity is still asleep.

He looks over to the television that is still tuned to the news. He has woken up early and still has some time before Linc comes to pick him up.

Thyme tries to close his eyes and fall back asleep, but after a few minutes of trying he gives up. He moves Chastity's legs off of his lap, carefully so as not to wake her and he stands and stretches. He goes upstairs and into the bathroom, looks around for mouthwash, sees an empty bottle, and then he picks up his toothbrush and brushes his teeth.

He goes down the stairs, and finds his sweatshirt and his camera and whispers into Chastity's ear, "I'm going out for a walk before Linc gets here."

She mumbles something that he doesn't understand and smiles in her sleep. He rubs her forehead, and then walks to the front door, unlocks it, and quietly leaves.

He walks down the sidewalk and turns left to begin his morning walk.

Across the street, Stan is awake and watching the video on his phone. When he hears a door close, he looks out the window and sees Momma's bastard son walking down the sidewalk. He watches as Thyme goes out of sight, and then he keeps watching about five minutes and then goes down the stairs in the vacant house and out the back door, stepping over the smashed glass from last night.

He goes to the side of the garage, and watches across the street for another five minutes.

Then he crosses the street and walks up Chastity's sidewalk without even looking around. He pauses at the door for a moment, and then he checks the handle, and finds it unlocked; he opens it a little, listens, and then walks in and quietly shuts the door back behind him; he doesn't lock it now either.

He walks by the room where Chastity is sleeping on the sofa, and he lingers there, watching her, listening to her slightly snore as she inhales and exhales.

He turns and walks into the kitchen, it has a lingering bacon smell and he finds a joint on the countertop and lights up with a lighter he finds and takes a few tokes on it before it starts to burn him and then he tosses it into the sink, which is half filled with water and dirty frying pans.

He opens one drawer and then closes it, and then opens another and takes out a knife, looks at it, and then puts it back into the same drawer and takes out another knife. He likes this one. He closes the drawer. He holds the knife and looks around the room for another joint roach, but doesn't find one.

He holds the lighter in his hand.

He flicks it and it lights the first try, and he keeps the lighter lit until it begins to burn his finger, the whole time walking slowly and quietly out of the kitchen and down the hall towards where Chastity is sleeping, soundly.

He stands in front of her, and without a pause, he holds the hot lighter into her neck and she wakes with a scream.

He drops himself down onto her; she's been sleeping in her usual outfit, just socks and a t-shirt. He's on top of her and he's holding the hot lighter to her neck, he drops the knife and covers her mouth with his left hand, and then drops the lighter and moves his right hand down between her legs, and begins to force his fingers into her.

She bites his fingers and he moves his hand from her mouth, all the while keeping his other hand between her legs; he spits into her mouth, and then hits her in the mouth with his left hand. Then, as she tries to kick him, he quickly undoes his belt, unbuttons his pants, and unzips his fly, he removes his hand from inside her long enough to pull down his pants and she can see he's erect, and he starts to lean into her; she starts to kick and struggle all the more.

She's blistering on the neck from the lighter, she's bleeding from her lips from where he hit her, and she's stinging between her legs where he's shoved his fingers.

She has a free arm, and for the first time she reaches down and touches a man; she grabs his testicles and squeezes with all her might. He shouts "Fairyblood!" and lifts his knee, ramming her under the jaw; she's bleeding more and crying now.

She lets go of his balls, and he grabs her hands with his. She's holding her legs together as hard as she can now that he's moved his fingers from her. He moves her arms together so he is holding both of her skinny wrists with one of his hands. With the other, he rubs his erection and then pries her legs apart, and then hits her in the mouth again; there's blood running down her face and neck and making the top of her t-shirt red; he leans in, smiling, getting ready to force his way inside her, and the front door opens and then slams shut and he thinks he hears a dog growl.

Thyme heard the shouts when he was on the sidewalk, and he runs in holding his camera by the strap and swinging it around above his head three times, four times, then five time and finally the heavy camera swings towards Stan right as he's about to enter Chastity and the camera crashes into Stan's teeth and nose, there's a sickening snapping sound and blood gushes from his nose, both nostrils, and his lips are bleeding.

Stan stumbles backwards and glares at Thyme. He spits a broken tooth towards him, then kicks Chastity once more and quickly grabs the kitchen knife from the sofa, and lunges towards Thyme, sinking the knife into Thyme's soft stomach. Thyme falls to the ground and Stan kicks him and runs out the front door as Chastity is screaming and running over to Thyme.

Thyme passes out feeling a dog licking his face.

Chastity hears Linc's big truck coming down the street.

Stan is looking back towards the house, cursing and running, his chin and shirt covered with blood, his pants dangling around one of his legs, he's still semi-erect and he's running diagonally across the yard and not looking and he's running towards the street and just as he runs into the street he looks to his left and Linc's 34,000 pound truck rams into Stan's chest and plows over him.

By the time the truck is over top of Stan, Stan is dead in the middle of the road; and the road is quiet now, there are no cars on it, the For Sale signs are rusting, and Stan is dead, just like that, dead.

He never lay dying; he just died, just like that: Slap!

Linc gets out, and hears Chastity screaming inside the house; he runs inside to see Chastity, near naked and bleeding and wailing, over top of Thyme, who is motionless on the floor, blood covered, and unconscious; Linc hears a dog whimpering.

Epilogue: [Beginnings]

An Erratic History of Thyme, Part Five

Now it's now, three months later or so, the winters gone and this is how it is:

Slap!

Linc hops down from the rear of his truck, he's wearing jeans in the summer and his tattooed knuckles are covered by gloves; he's wearing a plain white t-shirt, and sweating and swearing. He jumps down and walks over to a driveway, rolls the plastic bin to the truck, zones out in concentration, and the next thing he knows the bin is back where it used to be, and he's on the back of the truck, winking to women walking by, and then, Slap!

The truck goes two blocks this time and hangs a left, then goes another and Linc: Slap! And he hops down and walks towards the front of the truck. The window is open. Linc takes off his gloves and feels his pockets and then looks up to the window, and says, "I think I've lost my cell phone. Is it up there in the cab anywhere?"

The truck shifts gears into park; Linc waits on the street.

"No. Nothing."

"You sure?"

"I'm sure," Chastity says, "I saw you grab it when you got out."

"Uh. I think it's gone. I'm going to ride up with you the rest of the way." He walks in front of the truck, gazes down at the front fender, the one that slapped Stan, opens the passenger door, and climbs up. He slams it (Slap!), messes with the seatbelt, and looks over to Chastity and says, "Go on and drive to your house; I'll get in the driver's seat then," he winks over at Chastity, "I've got a date tonight."

Chastity smiles at him; then says, "Don't forget my paycheck, Linc."

"Ah, yes; Fridays."

She drives on and parks the truck in the middle of the street in front of her house; she shifts it into park and stomps the parking brake, then swings the door open and climbs down, not bothering to look left or right.

She looks up to the window, as Linc has slid across the seat in the cab and is framed by the window, looking down at her, smiling. She says, "Look," and she points to the house directly across the street from hers and the For Sale sign that had been growing weeds around it for months now, now has a Sale Pending sign, "And," and she points down the street, the way the truck was heading and there was another house with the same sign, Sale Pending, in the front yard.

Chastity smiles.

Linc smiles back and says, "Oh, here's your pay," and he holds some cash out the window.

"No."

"No?"

"No. You spend it tonight on your date. I don't need it. I just like helping; but I don't like having a job."

"Ah. See you tomorrow then?"

"See you tomorrow; good night, Linc. And, good luck, tonight."

"I don't need no luck . . . I'm the trash man, baby; baby, I'm the trash man." And he smiles, and he laughs out loud, the hardest he's laughed all day, and then for a moment he forgets that he's lost his cell phone, and Chastity smiles too, and then laughs aloud, and she turns, still smiling, and walks away from Linc's truck.

And he waits until she walks up the sidewalk, and she's at her front door, unlocking the handle with her keys, and Linc shifts his truck to drive, eases off the parking brake, and drives off to his date, where he'll look the woman in the eyes, blue or brown it doesn't matter, and say, "Baby, I'm the trash man; I'm the trash man, baby," and then he'll wave a waitress over with his tattooed knuckles. As he drives home that night, or hopefully the next morning, he'll do what he does every day: He'll drive his truck and wherever he goes, he'll be looking for Momma Exler, he's looking out for her on the sidewalk, drinking tea, and then turning around and walking away, forever.

Chastity opens the door and walks in; locking it behind her, as she always does now.

She's got a newspaper in her hand that she took from one of Linc's customers early this morning (she's a virgin, not an angel).

She kicks off her boots, sits on the steps leading upstairs, and she takes off her dirty socks; she can't wait to get some clean ones on. She's starving.

She walks to the kitchen; the lights are out and she turns them on with her elbow, rubbing her growling stomach with her right hand.

She sees a pair of clean white socks, men's socks, on the table with some of her clean clothes, and right there in the kitchen she pulls off her work pants, pulls down her underwear, strips off her t-shirt, keeping on only her bra as she doesn't see a clean one, and she pulls on a clean t-shirt and is sitting on the floor wrestling with a sock. Thyme, bearded and hair a little shaggier than last time we saw him, walks in slowly; he's in a little pain. He stops, looks down, and then smiles and backs out of the room.

By the time she gets both socks on and gets in the other room, he's sitting on the sofa, watching the news. He looks up to her and smiles, "Hey; how was today."

"Hot; really hot."

Thyme smiles.

She asks, "How are you feeling?"

"Sore. But not as sore as last week. I walked a mile and a half today."

She rubs his chest, then gently lifts up his t-shirt and looks at the scar in his stomach; she can see the incision scar, and she can where the stitches dotted the sides.

She asks him, "Did you see it again."

"All day."

"I wish I could see it."

"I wish you could too."

And Thyme, barefooted and bearded, grabs his camera from the counter. He rubs his stomach. He smiles through his beard and ignores the burning around his stomach's scar and the taste on his tongue, that bitter taste again, but he ignores it and it goes away sooner or later.

And he walks over to the window, and he takes a picture of the empty street in front of the house, in front of Chastity's house. And after the camera clicks, he keep looking at the street again, smiling.

He walks back across the room to Chastity.

He hands her the camera.

She looks down, and smiles, rubs her eyes, and smiles again.

"It's unreal."

"It is," he responds.

"Right where Linc's truck hit him, he's that blur, he's that shadow in the street, and that's a dog attacking him, biting him?"

"I see it every day. The ghost of a dog."

"The ghost of your dog?"

"The ghost of a dog."

"Biting him?"

"Biting the heck out of him; I told Momma he'd end up in hell someday."

"Have you seen Momma?"

"Not again; have you?"

"No," she pauses, "Tell me about what you can see in the street again; tell me what the dog is doing to that freak."

"A dog runs over, I can hear his tags, I can smell his fur, he runs over and he drags Stan from the ground up, from his neck, and then turns and rips into his neck. It's too much, even for a blur of an image."

"You see this every day, don't you."

"Yes."

"Does Stan scream?"

"Yes."

"And is it your dog?"

"It's just a dog."

"Tell me, Thyme."

"Yeah; it is. It's him."

"But you never see Momma again?"

"I've smelled her tea."

"And does that make you feel better?"

"Yeah; it makes me feel better; I feel good now, just thinking about it."

This is then, now, and this is how it is: He smiles, and closes his eyes for a minute, then two, dreaming about being a child and finding three pennies in the pocket of his favorite pants.

And he already feels good.

His dog had a name, the one that lived with him years ago, the one that protects him still; the dog had a name, and Thyme remembers what it was, but that was years ago.

"Do you know what I call things like that?"

"No; what?"

"Painkiller ghosts."

Get Published, Inc!
Thorofare, NJ 08086
07 April, 2010
BA2010097